THE ENLIGHTENMENT

BOOK 2 OF THE BLOODMOON WARS SERIES (A PARANORMAL SHIFTER ROMANCE SERIES)

SARA SNOW

ELINOR

I clenched my fists to stop my hands from trembling. Connor, now in his wolf form, was looking at Will with murder in his black eyes while I stood there, panicked. Large droplets of rain fell around us as thunder rumbled loudly above.

The sensation of having Will's lips on mine faded, washed away by the realization that my world was about to come crumbling down.

An Alpha-born werewolf—yes, me—caught kissing a vampire. If anyone ever found out about this, life as I knew it would be over. My actions would bring disgrace to the Blackwood name and subject our pack to ridicule. And worse, if Connor didn't kill Will, my father surely would. Then he'd probably banish me from the pack.

What have I done?

Connor growled as he lowered his head to the ground, his fur ruffling as the surrounding wind blew stronger. I looked at Will and frowned at the calm expression on his face. He didn't seem bothered or the least bit frightened. Instead, he just stood there and stared at Connor without even blinking.

Connor bared his fangs.

I stepped forward, my hands raised. "Connor, listen to me. You didn't need to signal the others. I'm not in danger. Please, let me explain what you just saw."

He growled at me and snapped his teeth. It was clear he wasn't interested in listening to my explanation. He rushed forward with a guttural growl. Beside me, Will became a blur, and before I could stop him, he ran at Connor. I watched in horror as the two men—or rather, one vamp and one wolf—collided.

My hand flew to my mouth as Connor's large teeth missed Will's throat by an inch.

"Connor! Will! Stop this!" I yelled, but neither of them was listening to me. "Please stop!"

As the Beta of my pack, it was Connor's job to keep the peace. While my father sat at the head of our pack, Connor was at the very end, keeping everything together. He held immense power, carrying out my father's orders and overseeing the pack when my father was away.

He howled the moment he'd found me with Will. More wolves from my pack would arrive any minute. I reached behind me to remove my dress. Maybe I could end the fight by shifting and getting in between them.

I looked up when I heard a loud whimper—Will had thrown Connor against the trunk of a tree. I watched as the pack Beta slid down the trunk to the ground, but he was back on his feet swiftly. He snarled loudly as he circled Will, his eyes never leaving Will's face.

He was obviously looking for an opening to attack, but

even with Will's back to me, I realized there wouldn't be one. There was a dark aura around Will that I'd never seen before. He stood there, rooted in one place as Connor circled him.

Connor rushed forward. To my surprise, he froze mid-attack. I frowned as I watched him. Connor was still looking straight at Will, but he didn't move a muscle. Will took one step forward and then another, and my frown deepened.

Will spoke, his words a mumbled whisper not even I was able to hear.

What in Goddess's name is he doing?

My hand fell to my side as I forgot about shifting. What was happening, and why had the fight stopped so suddenly? My confusion increased further when Will turned away from Connor and began walking towards me.

Behind him, Connor shook his head for a moment, then closed his eyes and lifted his head up to the sky, howling long and hard. He was telling the wolves he'd previously summoned that all was well and there was no need for them to come.

My eyes moved back and forth between him and Will.

"What's going on?" I asked Will as he drew closer. "What did you do?"

He said nothing in response as he walked towards the cliff, his hand brushing against mine as he passed me.

"Will?"

He strolled off the cliff without so much as a glance backward.

What the hell?

I turned around to find that Connor had already shifted into his human form. He pinched the bridge of his nose for a moment, his brows tightly knitted. "Connor? A-are you okay?"

He looked up, and his hand fell away from his face as he nodded. "Yes, I'm fine." He glared at me as his lips tightened, and my eyes widened. "What the hell were you doing? I thought you were going to fall over the cliff. Have you completely lost your mind?"

Um, what?

I said nothing, just stared at him in confusion. Did he hit his head or something during the fight?

He arched a brow at me as if I was the one acting out of character. "I thought you had slipped . . ." He shook his head as he looked down at his bare chest and then at his ripped shirt on the ground. "You're buying me another shirt."

"So . . . you thought I was going to fall off the cliff?" I asked hesitantly.

He nodded. "Yeah, I was patrolling the woods when I picked up on your scent. Why are you so far off our territory anyway? Come on, let's go."

He turned to leave, but I was still in shock and unable to move. What had Will done to him? It was as if someone had wiped and replaced his memory. Were vampires capable of doing something like that?

I remembered a rumor circulating a few years ago saying vampires were capable of compelling their victims to make them compliant. There were so many stories about vampires, nobody was really sure what was true and what was not.

But compulsion was the only answer I could come up with right now. What else could it have been?

I glanced at the cliff behind me and listened to the sound of the rushing waves rolling up from below. I'd only known

Will for a short time, but he'd gotten under my skin so quickly and so easily. Yet I knew so little about him. I reached up and touched my lips, closing my eyes.

I came to our spot tonight to tell him we couldn't see each other anymore—that I was now promised to another. And then he'd kissed me.

I opened my eyes and groaned with annoyance. Because I'd kissed him back. I'd wanted it—craved it—and now that it was over, I wanted more.

There was nothing to be done for it now. I turned around to follow Connor, lost in thought as we walked to my house in silence. One thought kept replaying in my mind in a constant loop. Will had saved my life, and after that, I'd been unable to get him off my mind. Had he compelled me to believe I had feelings for him?

This was probably why vampires and werewolves didn't mix. Actually, this was probably why vampires and *any* species didn't mix. I sighed as my house came into view.

Again, I wondered . . . what if my feelings weren't real? What if Will had compelled me to want to be with him?

And if that was the case, what was I going to do about it?

Skye

I dropped the potatoes I just bought into the bag that Cyrus was carrying for me. We walked from vendor to vendor, and soon, I only had one item left to get.

"There is literally no one selling peaches," I grumbled

under my breath as I looked around the market. "I can't leave without them."

"It's getting late, Skye. I can return tomorrow to get some for you," Cyrus offered, but I shook my head. Peaches were my absolute favorite fruit.

"You know I can't leave without them. Mother said she'd make pie if I brought some home," I grumbled. He sighed heavily.

I arched a brow at him, at the annoyance on his face, and cleared my throat. "You offered to come with me, Cyrus. You could have waited for me at the house."

"Such an appreciative woman," he growled sarcastically as he walked off. I followed him, still scanning the market for peaches.

"I see you two are still inseparable," a voice said from behind me. I turned around to see Yathleen—an elf known for her potent healing herbs—smiling at me. "I've yet to get used to your friendship—a demon and a werewolf." She shook her head, then narrowed her eyes. "Where is the third?"

"Oh, Elinor is at home. She's been pretty busy lately," I answered.

Yathleen smiled again. "I see."

"So, do you have anything for me?" I grinned.

Her long white hair blew wildly in the wind while my short dark curls only moved a little. And her milky white skin was a distinct contrast to mine. We looked like we lived in two different worlds.

"Of course," she answered in her soft, eerie elvish voice.

She reached into the basket in her hand and pulled out a bunch of herbs tied together with a string. Even though werewolves usually healed on their own, training to become a pack doctor included learning about herbal medicines. Some wounds were beyond a werewolf's natural healing abilities, and we occasionally needed to use supplemental treatments.

"Thank you," I told her as I gave the herbs to Cyrus, who was waiting impatiently behind me. He was usually easygoing, so I couldn't help but wonder what his problem was. I paid Yathleen, and we said our goodbyes.

"Hey, what's going on with you?" I asked him.

He shook his head. "Nothing, I . . ." He sighed. "I need to feed."

My brows arched at that as heat crept up my cheeks. As an incubus, Cyrus was forced to feed on the sexual desires of others in order to survive. Of course, the moment he said those words, I instantly recalled him feeding on me—and the kiss we shared afterward.

I cleared my throat. "I see. Well, um, we can take care of that when we get home."

His chuckle stopped me in my tracks. I glared up at him.

"You're cute when you get flustered, Skye." He leaned in, his face just inches from mine. "I can go without feeding tonight, but I need to take care of it soon. But look, I think what you're looking for is right behind you."

I turned around, suddenly needing some distance between us. "Oh, there they are."

I walked away without saying another word, but I could feel his eyes on me. Cyrus and me talking about things like this out in the open could be a problem. No one knew about the feelings we had for each other, and it had to stay that way. Although my pack openly welcomed Cyrus despite his demon heritage, a romantic relationship between us would push the boundaries of that goodwill past the breaking point.

"Cyrus!" I heard a small voice call out as I took the bag of peaches from the vendor I had been chatting with.

I turned around and found Cyrus circled by kids. They were all talking at once, each one wanting his full attention. I remained where I was as they bombarded him with questions until a female centaur and elf joined them. I smiled at a little boy who was sitting on the back of the centaur, stealing shy glances at Cyrus.

The half-woman, half-horse supernatural used her tail to gently slap the boy on her back. "Still too shy to speak to Cyrus, are you, David?"

Cyrus smiled as he moved closer to better see the human boy, who only tried to hide further. I chuckled to myself and Cyrus turned to me. His piercing gray eyes stared into mine for a moment and my heart skipped a beat before I hurriedly looked away.

I'd known for a long time that Cyrus spent hours at an orphanage for both the human children and supernatural ones here in town during his free time. But I'd never actually seen him with the kids. I watched him smile as he picked up a boy and girl, balancing one on either hip easily.

It was obvious he loved children, and they adored him. Even the young pups in my pack were obsessed with him. It was just more proof that Cyrus was special. He had saved my life back when we were kids and had earned a place among my pack, though he was a demon. Every day, he proved that he was one of a kind.

Yet I knew he still had those primal demon urges. But didn't we all have a little darkness within us?

After a moment, the elf and woman who ran the orphanage pried the children away from Cyrus. Waving his goodbyes to them, he returned to my side.

"I have an idea," I said, ignoring the way he narrowed his eyes. "Do you remember telling me you felt as if you don't have a purpose here?" His eyes narrowed further as he took the bag of peaches from me. "Well, I think you should teach the pups in our pack."

He paused. "Come on, Skye, don't play around. I thought you were being serious there for a minute."

"I am! Just hear me out, okay? You're great with children, so you'd be a natural teacher. Why *not* help the pups in my pack? They don't start learning about dark creatures until they're in their teens. And even then, they only learn to fear those creatures—or worse, hate them, even though they see you, *a demon,* around all the time. You can educate them about all supernaturals while also showing them that not all creatures classified as dark are evil."

I could see the wheels turning in his head as he glanced from side to side. "I admit, that's not a bad idea. But Alpha Grayson will have to agree to something like that. Sure, I'm allowed onto pack territory freely and all, but I'm not exactly a part of the pack."

I rolled my eyes. "My mother raised you on pack territory. You're one of us, and you know it. I'm sure Alpha Grayson will see that my idea is brilliant because, hey, *I'm* brilliant. Now, I think I spotted a merchant selling grapes over there. Wait here, will you?"

Recently, Cyrus had confessed to me he felt he added nothing to the pack, that he had no real purpose. True, he didn't have a job per se and was more of a wanderer. Still, I'd be damned if I allowed him to think he didn't belong with us. His habit of not feeding even when he was starving drove me crazy enough as it was.

Escaping the Demon Realm as a child and being raised by werewolves had been hard on Cyrus. When his urge to feed first emerged, he had to leave us. Elinor, my mother, and I were at a loss as to how to help him, and we were also at risk of being affected by his uncontrollable power. We had no choice but to let him go. After he returned several months later in full control of his abilities and thirst, he refused to discuss where he'd been and what he'd done while he was gone. But he'd found his control somewhere.

Over time, I decided it was best I didn't know. But if he became a teacher and worked around children daily, he'd have no choice but to remain fed. Even though he didn't grow up in the Demon Realm, he was well-educated and well-traveled. The pups would learn a lot from him.

A tingle went down my spine at the memory of us lying on the floor of my house.

I shook my head as night drew closer and darkness steadily settled over the world.

"Thank you," I said as I took the grapes from the elderly human merchant.

She nodded, and I walked back to Cyrus. The first vendor I had come across had been selling her grapes for far too much money. So, after asking Cyrus to wait on me, I was forced to make my way through an alley to the other side of the market. That had been over ten minutes ago. Still, since Cyrus hadn't shown up yet to drag me home, I guessed I was safe from his wrath.

I just know it pisses him off, though. I really didn't plan to stay out this long.

"Hey gorgeous, need some company?"

I stopped in my tracks, turning around quickly to see two humans walking towards me. I rolled my eyes as I shook my head. "You fools have a death wish? Go mess with someone else."

Even someone without heightened senses like mine would've been able to smell the stench of alcohol on the two men as they kept moving towards me, wearing dirty rags that somehow passed for clothing. "I said get lost!" I growled. My brown eyes changed to black as my fangs elongated, and they took a step back, finally seeming to realize the danger they were in.

Supernaturals and humans in this town lived in harmony most of the time, but occasionally someone stepped out of line and caused friction between the two species. I had no intention of being the one to start anything, even if these fools were the aggressors.

My nostrils flared as I picked up on the scent of a third human, but when I spun around, it was too late. I gasped as something sharp pricked my neck. When I quickly pulled the object out of my skin, I saw it was a needle coated in a green substance.

My eyes fell on the human who had snuck up on me, his wide grin revealing rotten teeth.

"You men are scum—" I said, but before I could finish, my legs buckled. My eyes became blurry as I fell to the ground. I paled at the sound of the sickening laughter coming from the three men.

No, no . . . this can't be happening!

I tried to call on my wolf to shift, but the numbness in my legs was steadily spreading to the rest of my body. A gust of wind blew dust into my eyes, making me squint as I fell helplessly to the side, my head hitting the ground hard.

A guttural growl echoed around me, and I fought against the urge to close my eyes. The sound wasn't the growl of a werewolf, but an anguished sound that made goosebumps sprout on my skin. Then red wings came into view.

I mustered all my rapidly diminishing strength. "Cy-Cyrus." It came out no louder than a whisper.

A burst of heat engulfed me. I forced my eyes open as a man on fire fell to the ground a few steps away from me. His frantic screams filled the night.

"You fuckers! How dare you hurt her!"

I frowned inwardly—that deep baritone voice sounded familiar, but at the same time, it was like nothing I'd ever heard before. Even with my body numb, I felt a chill in the air. It was seeping into my skin. I fought to move my head, and finally, Cyrus came into view.

My heart skipped a beat at the man—no, the beast—standing before me. This wasn't a form he'd ever transformed into before—not one I'd ever seen, at least. He seemed taller, his wingspan wider than ever, and his fiery-red eyes appeared almost sinister. This wasn't the Cyrus I knew and loved.

I watched in fascination as the black tattoos covering his body all seemed to be moving towards his face.

The man he was holding up by the throat, the one who had given me a shot of something dangerous, was gasping for air. Cyrus's head tilted to the side as he watched the man die slowly, his legs dangling high above the ground.

Cyrus.

There was a crackling sound, and I cringed as I realized it was the sound of my attacker's bones breaking. Cyrus had released him, but he remained suspended in the air. The man's legs and arms bent and twisted in unnatural directions as his panicked screams filled the surrounding air.

"You will never lay hands on another woman again," Cyrus said, his voice thundering through the alley.

If I'd been able to move or speak, I would have gasped as the man exploded into a cloud of dust before my very eyes. Unable to take any more, I let my eyes finally close. As I felt the warmth coming from Cyrus's body, I whimpered.

"Stay with me, Skye." He picked me up. Then we rose into the sky. "Please, just stay with me."

I welcomed the darkness.

2

CYRUS

A FEW WEEKS PRIOR

I inhaled deeply and noted how different the air was in the Underworld compared to Earth. Here, power vibrated within the air, almost as if it was begging to be siphoned and used by the demon inhabitants. The air on Earth held less magic, felt lighter. Although I could pull less power from in the air on Earth, I still missed it. And I wanted to go back, now. I had no interest in playing the devoted son at my father's ball.

And that was the problem. Here in the Demon Realm, those who possessed the most power felt the weight of the magic in the air more. And I felt it so much, I could hardly breathe.

I watched as demon after demon made their way into my father's castle. I could hear the music from inside the towering monstrosity easily, along with the loud chatter and laughter of people I didn't know.

I inhaled deeply and exhaled heavily. This night would end badly. How could it not? I was the Demon King's son, but I lived on Earth. No doubt someone was going to say something to piss me off.

My father had a lot of children. But because I'd chosen to live elsewhere, I was the notorious one. Although my mother, with her endless rambling about me one day taking over her Legion of demons, didn't help matters. Still, I had no interest in becoming the next embodiment of Lust.

I slowly started making my way towards the dark castle. Black clouds hung low above the stronghold as thunder rumbled in the distance. How dramatic! It wasn't as if the entire Demon Realm was this gloomy, but of course, the Demon King made his home on a mountain surrounded by lava.

I crossed the obsidian bridge as lava poured on either side of it. Finally, I made it inside, surprised to discover that the inside looked nothing like I expected.

Yes, this was the first time I'd ever seen my father's home. My high and mighty sperm donor might have done his part to bring me into this world, but that was about the only thing he'd done for me. Besides, the children he'd sired outside of his marriage to the Demon Queen were of little interest to him. Everyone knew that. So why the sudden interest in me?

While darkness shrouded the castle outside, the inside was much brighter and smacked of luxury. Glistening crystals covered a massive chandelier hanging high above a grand entrance, providing brilliant illumination without any candles. The radiant light reflected off the pure white marble of the elegant double staircases to my left.

Immaculately dressed demons chatted amongst each other as they openly admired the luxurious surroundings.

All right, the sperm donor has taste. I'll give him that.

Since most of the guests were making their way to the second floor, I figured that had to be where the ballroom was. And the second floor was just as grand as the first. At the top of the marble staircase, I encountered a massive fountain with a life-sized sculpture of Queen Asura at its center. I'd never met the Demon Queen, but I'd heard rumors of her beauty.

Still, I'd thought she'd be taller. I walked away, supposing tonight I'd get to see her in person. I didn't expect to speak to my father, let alone get close to him or the Queen. The only reason I was here was to put in an appearance as mother wanted me to, then leave as soon as the opportunity arose.

"Wow, if it isn't Cyrus. How nice of you to grace us with your presence, brother."

I sighed, then turned around and came face-to-face with one of my positively delightful half-brothers. Orias, the second son of the King and Queen, wasn't the heir to the throne but acted as if he were. We'd only met a few times, but his hatred for me was clear. The feeling was mutual. His spoiled and entitled behavior made me sick, and I wasn't alone in thinking that. In fact, I was sure most of the nobles in the Demon Realm would agree with me.

"Half-brother," I corrected.

He waved his hand dismissively. "Of course, what else could you be?" His bald head reflected the light from above and was more than a little distracting. "I wasn't expecting to see trash like you here. You really didn't have to come tonight, Cyrus. No one would've missed you."

I tilted my head to the side and smiled. "I think those

succubi behind you are making fun of your hair . . . or lack of it." Sure enough, all three women erupted into laughter when he looked around. He narrowed his pale green eyes at me, but I didn't care. He wasn't worth my time. "Don't worry, Orias. I'm sure our father's ballroom is big enough that we won't have to breathe the same air."

Demons were stopping to watch our little altercation—exactly the situation I'd wanted to avoid. I turned to walk away when I felt him grab my elbow. My rage flared, and I clenched my fists once and then released them. I wasn't about to let him provoke me. So I took a deep breath and tried to calm down instead.

His face twisted with hate. "There it is . . . that fucking smug attitude. You're not as strong as you think, Cyrus. And don't think you're special just because you inherited our father's wings. You're nothing."

Does this man-child really think he has what it takes to one day be the Demon King?

I said nothing in response as I stared at his fingers still wrapped around my arm. I pulled out of his hold, then glared at him, letting him know with a glance just how little I thought of him. Though he was on the bulky side and had strong fire magic, this fool wasn't strong enough to beat me if it came to a fight.

And he knew it.

He'd hated me since the moment we'd first met—the moment he realized that I inherited our father's signature red wings . . . and he hadn't. "I don't have time for this, Orias. Go have a hissy fit about some other unnecessary shit elsewhere. I thought you would have grown up by now."

"Who do you think you are?" he growled as his eyes changed to black.

The surrounding demons gasped, and a new power filled the air. Behind Orias, a woman appeared out of thin air, her red hair flowing down to her ankles. She looked at Orias and then at me before her red-painted lips slowly curved into a smile.

"Mother?" Orias said, then turned around and slowly bowed his head. All the demons around us did the same.

I bowed my head as well when suddenly, I felt a hand on my shoulder. How had she moved so quickly?

"Don't pick fights you can't win," she whispered, her voice soft and melodic.

Huh?

As I looked up, my brows furrowed. I realized that, while her hand was on my shoulder, she was looking at Orias. His green gaze, so like hers, fell to her hand on my shoulder, and his eyes slowly widened with shock.

"Mom, what are you doing?" he asked through clenched teeth as the Queen's hand fell away from my shoulder.

"This is a party, Orias—your father's party. What are you doing, causing a scene like this? Leave and come back when you're thinking clearly. Or would you rather I tell your father you've chosen this moment to have one of your tantrums?"

Orias's face turned red with rage, but he turned and walked away, the red cloak he was wearing billowing behind him. I shook my head as I turned to the Queen and found her eyes already on me, a puzzling smile on her lips.

"So, you're Cyrus . . ." Her eyes roamed up and down my body. "It's so nice to finally meet you."

"Likewise, Queen Asura. I'm surprised you'd trouble yourself to know someone like me," I said, interlocking my fingers behind my back.

She chuckled, then held her hand out for us to walk together, the tail of her red dress trailing behind her on the ground. Behind us, her guards—giant hound demons in human form—were watching everyone's move, including mine. If anyone dared to attack or anger the Queen, those guards would transform into massive dogs with teeth and claws powerful enough to bite or tear through steel itself.

"I consider it my duty to know about all the children my husband has brought into this world." The smile on her lips was constant, and her voice never rose above a whisper. "You, however, are peculiar. I see a lot more of him in you than in my son Orias."

I gritted my teeth. "Forgive me, Your Majesty, but I'm nothing like my father."

She chuckled and shook her head. "You don't even know him. How can you make such a statement?"

We came to a stop before towering golden double doors that led into a grand hall. Thousands of demons were inside, but the loud chatter and clinking glasses stopped the moment the Queen and I appeared at the door. She held her hand out to me, and I raised my arm for her to hold.

"I'll be watching you, Cyrus. You have significant power." Then she took a step forward and I did the same, all the while cursing my bad luck. I'd gone from hoping I'd go unnoticed by blending into the crowd, to having all eyes on me the moment I arrived.

The crowd before us suddenly parted, creating a path

straight to the King at the very end of the hall. The Queen sashayed her way through the crowd to a chorus of compliments from her subjects, forcing me to escort her halfway to the King's throne before her guards moved me to the side.

I figured that would be as close as I'd get to my father, since there was another line of guards keeping the crowd away from the King as well.

He was sitting atop his throne, in all his golden-cloak-wearing glory. His black hair was long and straight, and while his Queen wore a large dazzling crown, he had nothing on his head. Even sitting down, it was obvious he was staggeringly tall. I guessed him to be about 7'2" in height.

Thinking of the Queen's words, I studied my father, quickly noticing how much my face shape resembled his. Our noses were both slightly crooked. Of course, I knew there would be some resemblance between us, but I hadn't expected this much.

I look like a younger version of him. In fact, if I let my hair grow, I'd be the spitting image of him.

His red eyes remained on me from the moment I had entered with his wife on my arm. Only once before had I seen this man, when I was but a child. But now, I was fully grown and able to hold his stare without backing down.

Finally, the Queen took her seat beside the King, and I walked away happily, making my way through the crowd of demons, who all still had their eyes on me. Then suddenly, someone called my name. I held back a growl as I turned and spotted my mother waving at me. Her silver dress—if the garment could actually be called a dress, since it only covered her breasts, arms, and thighs—was glistening from the crystals sewn onto it.

"My boy," she gushed as she finally reached me and kissed my cheeks. "You look so handsome!"

"You picked out what I'm wearing, Mother. I found it in my room along with your note."

She shrugged. "Well, of course, I wouldn't let you come here dressed the way you usually are when you're . . ." She sighed and rolled her eyes. ". . . on Earth."

I couldn't stop myself from laughing. "You looked like you were going to throw up just from saying the word 'Earth.'"

"I was," she gritted out. I shook my head, still chuckling.

She winked at me with a smile before leaning forward and moving a strand of perfectly curled black hair behind her ear. "What were you just doing with the Queen? What were you two talking about?"

"You waste no time, do you, Mother?" I asked. She smiled sweetly, even though we both knew there was nothing sweet about her. This woman had a black hole where her heart should be. "We weren't talking about anything interesting."

"The Queen singled you out. She must have had a reason," she argued. I only shrugged.

She ran her hand down the sleeve of the black cotton shirt she had picked out for me. She'd painted her pointy nails in black and decorated them with crystals that matched the ones on her dress—and the ones that ran down the sides of my cloak. To an outsider, it would appear as if my mother loved me. But I knew better. I was only special to her because of who my father was. She'd do anything for the King. Hell, if he told her to cut her arm off right now, I'd bet she'd do it without a moment of hesitation.

I looked around the room and wondered how many demons would say no if asked to do the same.

"You look pale, Cyrus." She narrowed her eyes and pressed her lips together. "You need to feed. I told you to take care of that before you came. I even sent three humans to your room."

"I'm not hungry," I replied almost immediately. "And I sent your pets away."

The three human girls had reeked of the other incubi they'd been with. I watched as my mother's face became expressionless, even as the veins on her neck began to throb. I knew what she was thinking, but she couldn't say it—not with everyone around. She hated the fact that I lived on Earth, that I chose to live with werewolves over my own family. And even more, she hated that I refused to lose myself and become the sex-crazed person she was. Just because I was required to feed on the desire of others to survive didn't mean I couldn't exercise a little self-control about how and when and who I did it with.

"Valencia?"

My mother and I looked towards the person who had called her name. When I saw who it was, I knew another confrontation was about to happen. Draped in a deep green cloak with white feathers around the hood, one of the other Sins like my mother, Greed, looked me up and down with his observant emerald eyes before drifting over to my mother.

"Hello, my dear." The tall, thin man bent forward and kissed her cheek. "You look stunning, as always."

"Aw, thank you, Shax," my mother replied. As the rich sound of piano music filled the air, Shax's attention landed on me.

"I wasn't expecting to see you here," he said, running his fingers through his dark brown hair.

Shax had always had a thing for my mother. And as the embodiment of the Sin Greed, he thought she should belong to him and him only. Of course, she'd slept with him, but considering she was a succubus and the Sin Lust, that meant nothing. She wasn't exactly choosy about who she slept with. He wasn't anything special to her, but he refused to see it. And he hated me for the attention she gave me.

"Now, now, be nice, boys," she quickly intervened. "This is a party, after all. Don't make a scene."

Shax ignored her, his green eyes turning black. *Here it comes.* I looked at my mother. "Why did you make me come here, again?"

"You don't deserve to be the next leader of your mother's Legion. You don't care about the Demon Realm at all. You've lived . . . on Earth—" He practically spat the word. "—all your life. So why should you receive such an honor?" He stepped closer to me and my mother stepped back, a grin on her lips. Despite what she had said about not making a scene, this was beyond entertaining for her.

"You're wasting your time," I answered. "I don't care what you or anyone here thinks of me. My mother asked me to attend, so here I am."

I saw his hand rise but sluggishly, as if the world around me was moving at a slower speed than I was. Shax always had quite the temper, despite being the Sin of Greed and not Wrath. Ironically, Wrath was usually pretty calm.

My wings burst from my back and loud gasps filled the room as demons scattered to avoid being knocked over by them. I could see Shax visibly rethinking his plan of grabbing me, as his hand froze mid-air. *Good.* I folded my wings behind me and stepped forward, pointedly ignoring Shax as I walked around him.

I left Shax and my mother behind, eyeing a bottle of wine across the room. I rarely drank, but I was going to need something to get through this night. There was no going back for me now, no blending into the crowd and silently leaving.

I ignored the whispers swirling around me—demons commenting on my wings, wondering why I had them, guessing why I'd come tonight. It was not lost on me how confusing this must have been for demons who didn't know who I was. First, I entered with the Queen on my arm, and then I flashed my wings, which, according to demon lore, I shouldn't even have.

Only the King, his first son and heir to the throne, and the third crowned prince sported red wings—the symbol of the Demon Realm. And then I showed up, the son of one of his booty calls, a son who few other demons were even aware of. One who lived on Earth instead of being glued to the King's side for his approval like the rest of his kids.

It seemed like people down here didn't understand how the inheritance of traits worked. Any of Father's children could have inherited his wings. Just because red wings were rarely seen outside the royal family didn't mean it never happened.

Okay, so I could understand Orias hating my guts for it. He was the only crowned prince who didn't get wings.

I got myself a glass of wine and leaned against the wall by an open window. The loud music drowned out the sound of thunder outside, but at least it meant I didn't have to hear the barely-concealed gossip about me that was surely making the rounds by now.

Loud drums echoed through the grand hall, and everyone turned their attention to the door as demons in gold masks started making their way inside. Behind them, women wearing similar gold masks were dancing to the beat of the drums.

Swirling gold lines twisted around their every curve, while a thin, sheer fabric covered their breasts. However, the rest of the women's bodies were on display for all to see. Loud whistles echoed among the guests as the girls disbursed within the crowd, their hips moving wildly with the rapid beat of the drums.

"Well, well, look who it is."

I tilted my head to the side as a man with thick blond hair and blue eyes grinned at me. I narrowed my eyes at him, wondering why he looked so happy to see me, especially considering I had no idea who he was.

He came to a stop beside me and tapped his glass against mine. "How long has it been, brother?"

I blinked as I realized who was standing before me. "Theanos?" I guessed, and his smile grew wider.

"In the flesh," he replied as he finished his wine in one swig, though some of it ran down his long chin. He threw the glass through the window and wiped his chin, then chuckled. "I was hoping you'd turn up. But I hadn't imagined you'd be the center of attention."

"Yeah, you and me both," I grumbled, and he laughed.

Before I had left the Demon Realm and moved to Earth when I was a boy, Theanos had been the only sibling I could stand, the only one who'd ever been kind to me. Because he was the son of a Dragon King, our mother used to drive him crazy, the way she did to me now that I was no longer the frail child I used to be. Once it became known that I had inherited the King's wings, I quickly became her new obsession. I liked it a lot better when she'd focused all her attention on her dragon-born son—though I doubted Theanos missed the attention.

I never thought I'd miss the days when my mother didn't give a damn about me.

"It's nice to see you, Cyrus," he said in a low voice.

I nodded. "It's nice to see you too, Theanos," I answered truthfully. I was thankful there was at least one person in this place that didn't hate me.

The tempo of the drums changed, and Theanos and I watched as the palace staff led more humans into the hall. Both women and men were naked, dancing without a care in the world that they were being offered up as playthings and food.

I swallowed hard as my hand twitched by my side.

Maybe I should have fed before coming here.

I could smell the desire rolling off the humans in waves, and I quickly looked away as an incubus grabbed a nearby woman and sank his fangs into her throat. My kind didn't feed on blood, but biting our victims allowed us to introduce a chemical into their system that heightened their arousal even further.

It was also how we made our mark once we decided to take that path. Of course, marking wasn't a common practice, since most incubi and succubi preferred to remain single.

"Are you going to feed?" Theanos asked.

I shook my head. Living among the wolves in Skye's and Elinor's pack had forced me to control myself, restraining my hunger to the point where I became ill. Yes, I knew that it wasn't healthy, but my feelings for Skye had played a large part in preventing me from feeding on anyone else.

I'd yet to tell her about my feelings, about what I'd felt for her ever since we were children. But I felt as if I'd betrayed her each time I had another woman beneath me. I never learned not to care about such things the way most demons do, since I grew up with wolves who dedicated themselves to one partner.

"In that case, I want to talk to you about something," he added. I nodded, thankful for the chance to get out of this place.

We made our way through the castle until the loud music and the feeding frenzy going on in the ballroom didn't seem so loud. I inhaled the scent of flowers as we entered a garden, trying to forget the sweet smell of sex we left behind.

I caught Theanos looking at me curiously after we found a bench to sit down on, so I stopped taking deep breaths and arched a brow. "What?"

He shook his head. "Nothing. I just wanted to talk to you about using your portal."

That piqued my interest, and I crossed my arms over my chest. It was common to find unmapped portals in the Demon Realm—gateways that could take you to any other realm. After finding one close to Skye's pack as a child, I spelled it so no one else could use it without my permission. It had taken me years to perfect the spell to the point where it would notify me if someone tried to break it.

"Why?" I asked.

His brows pulled together with frustration. "You and I are the only two sons Valencia has that are of royal blood. You got away . . . but I wasn't so lucky." He inhaled and held his head back to stare up at the black starry sky above us. "You and I think alike, but because of you, she keeps a close eye on me, watching me every time I go to Earth." He looked my way, and I nodded with understanding. He'd grown tired of her, too. "I *need* a break, Cyrus."

More than anyone, I understood the weight on Theanos's shoulders. Our mother wasn't plaguing him to be the next leader of her Legion, but being the second-born son of a Dragon King, she forced him to stay close—just in case. As the spare, he'd be next in line for the throne if anything happened to his half-brother, the heir.

"Sure," I answered. It would be nice to have him visit sometime. And I was sure the girls would like to meet him.

He was a little wild, maybe, but he was a good guy. At least, he had been when we were children. Maybe inviting him before knowing how much he'd changed was a bad idea, but having at least one person from my family on my side couldn't be a bad thing.

The towering form of the King appeared at the entrance of the garden, and Theanos and I fell silent.

"King Abraxas, is everything okay?" Theanos asked as he stood up and bowed in respect. I remained seated.

"Yes, of course, Theanos, thank you." His red eyes drifted to me. "I'd like to speak to my son."

My eyes lowered at that, and Theanos looked my way. "Of course," he replied and turned to leave but not before raising a curious brow my way.

"You don't have to leave, Theanos." King Abraxas raised his hand, and Theanos froze. "This won't take long."

Theanos looked from the King to me and then back again. "Okay."

We waited in silence for a moment. Then the King's lips curved with a smile. "You're not what I had expected. You're not the little boy I remember."

"That was many years ago," I answered as I finally stood up. "A lot has changed."

He nodded once in agreement. "I'm looking forward to the time you take over your mother's Legion. She speaks highly of you."

"I'm afraid I won't be her successor. My older brother Baxton is in line to be the next Sin," I replied, and his thick brow arched ever so slightly.

"Let me rephrase that." His voice was gravelly, as if he was growling each time a word left his lips. But as he stepped forward, his voice deepened. The air of calm that had surrounded him vanished, and Theanos and I got a glimpse of the powerful king he truly was.

His eyes abruptly flared and the dark power vibrating off his body grew almost stifling. "You're my son. You bear my wings as proof of that. No son of mine with your potential will be wasted among mortals. I'll give you three more years on Earth, but after that time, you'll return to me in the Underworld. Do you understand? If you still refuse to return —the way your mother has been telling me you're doing—I'll give you a reason to come back. And you won't like it."

I clenched my teeth at his blatant threat but remained quiet. Although I really wanted to take him down, I was no match for the Demon King in a fight. Not yet, and probably never. But I didn't like the threat to my family on Earth. There was no doubt in my mind that, like my mother, he wouldn't hesitate to hurt Skye or Elinor if it suited his personal agenda. Clearly, my mother had been telling him everything.

He turned to leave without waiting for my response. "My door is always open for you, my son. I'll be seeing you soon."

3

CYRUS

PRESENT

Skye's chest rose and fell slowly as she slept. She moaned a little, and a small crease appeared between her brows. I couldn't help wondering what she was dreaming about. At least she was asleep and not suffering anymore. Extracting the poison from her blood was a painful ordeal—for both of us.

I reclined in my chair, recalling the way those bastards had attacked her. She had been on the ground, so she probably hadn't noticed that their eyes were black—proof that they were possessed. My father's threat had echoed in my mind the moment I saw their eyes, and my rage had consumed me. I grew angry all over again just thinking about it, so I closed my eyes and took a deep breath to calm and center myself. Getting upset now wouldn't help her wake up. Nothing would, according to Nurse Hilary.

I almost lost her. Those scumbags almost took her from me.

I clenched and unclenched my fists repeatedly as I continued to watch her sleep. I would not tell her about my suspicions when she woke up. Because if I did, I'd have to tell her about what happened at my father's ball. And I wasn't ready for that yet.

She'd been asleep for two days now, but I refused to leave her side. Now that all the poison was out of her bloodstream, I knew she'd be okay. But whatever toxin had been in that injection had almost shut her body down, forcing her into a coma. If I hadn't found her when I did, she would have died.

I shook my head and sighed. Thinking about what might have happened wouldn't help with my rage. I looked towards the window and saw the sun slowly rising. I hadn't slept all night long. But I just couldn't—not with my thoughts running wild.

Skye and I had finally acknowledged our feelings for each other, but there was still so much she didn't know. So much she didn't know about *me*.

Three years. I only have three years left.

I thought again of the question Theanos posed before he left to head back to the Demon Realm after his visit. He had asked if I'd made my choice about Skye. I had told him that yes, I had every intention of making Skye mine and asking her to come with me to the Underworld.

I turned away from the window to stare at her, a feeling of doubt settling over me. What if she met her mate before I had to go back? Or what if she refused?

I wouldn't blame her if she said no. I'd be asking her to move with me to the Demon Realm, leaving Elinor, her mother, and her pack behind. But just this once, I had to be selfish. I needed her to come with me.

Because I couldn't see myself ever being with anyone else.

"Once you mark her, there is no turning back," Theanos had said.

"The day I leave, I'll have her by my side," I had replied. But was that wishful thinking?

"And if she says no?" he'd asked. "What if that's not what she wants or she meets her mate? What will you do? I've been watching you, Cyrus. You need to stop restraining yourself in feeding and in using your power. You might not want to accept it, but you *are* the son of the Demon King. Those red wings aren't the only things you inherited from him. You have his power . . . and his rage. If you keep holding yourself back the way you have been, you'll eventually explode. You'll try to let it go, but you'll end up losing total control."

I'd ignored Theanos's words at the time, but the rage that ripped through me when I saw Skye fall to the ground was like nothing I'd ever felt before. My thirst for vengeance was almost blinding. And for a minute, all I wanted to do was kill those men.

I'd had to take a few lives here before to defend myself against a dark creature or two, though I tried to avoid conflict whenever possible. But closing my eyes, I recalled the feeling of satisfaction I felt after watching that vermin explode. Those men got to Skye so easily . . . I had no choice anymore. I had to tell her everything.

"Wake up," I said out loud as the morning sun beamed through the window. I smiled as Skye's skin appeared to glow in the sun's rays. "We need to talk."

Elinor

The moment I heard Skye was finally awake, I was out of the house and on my way to hers. I got there in record time, my legs burning from running nonstop. Sure, our town wasn't without its issues, but humans attacking a werewolf the way those men had gone after Skye? That was unheard of.

"You moron!" I yelled, storming into her room. I found her sitting up in bed with Cyrus by her side. And despite the concern I felt when I entered the room, my heart swelled with joy at the small smile on her face.

"I'm okay, I swear!" she said, but I didn't want to listen to her. I just wanted to grab her and hug her and make sure she was really all right. Since Cyrus killed all the men who attacked her, there was no way of knowing exactly what they intended to do with Skye. But then, everyone knew there was a black market for supernatural creatures.

I ran across the room, then pulled her into a hug, brushing that troubling thought aside. "If you do that ever again, I'll be the one to put you into a coma." I pulled away and sat on her bed beside her. "We both will."

Cyrus nodded in agreement, and I noticed how much better he looked compared to a few days ago. He hadn't left Skye's side since he flew to the packhouse with her in his arms the night it had happened, startling everyone with the form he had been in.

Before he arrived, even my mother had felt a chill in the air, signaling strong darkness heading towards the pack. We thought we were under attack, but after Cyrus arrived with a wounded Skye, we realized what was happening. I'd never seen him look so ferocious before. It was as if he shifted into a creature of pure rage and darkness.

"How are you feeling?" I asked Skye, holding one of her hands while Cyrus held the other. "You need to be more careful. Our town is one of the more peaceful ones, but you know this crap happens from time to time. We're werewolves, but we're not immortal."

Skye frowned for a moment. "I know that. They just . . . took me by surprise. That's all."

When I first saw Skye after the attack and heard her faint heartbeat, I fell into a state of panic that I'd only ever felt once before—when I realized a vampire bit my friend Meeka during our examination to become Werewolf Guards. The sadness I saw in Meeka's eyes when she'd realized she was about to die still haunted my nightmares to this day.

My eyes burned with tears, and this time, Skye squeezed my hands.

I can't lose Skye—not now, not ever.

"Don't ever fucking do that again, woman! I mean it!" I looked at Cyrus and saw that his eyes were wet with unshed tears.

"I'll be right back," he said as he abruptly got up and left the room.

Skye and I looked at each other, understanding the mix of fear and relief he must be feeling. Cyrus always kept his emotions locked up tight. We rarely saw him sad or upset. But this was something else, and we all knew it.

"He'll be okay," I said as Skye's eyes filled with sadness. She probably felt horrible for scaring everyone. "He was just worried like the rest of us were. But you're okay, and that's what matters."

"If he hadn't been there . . ." she started, trailing off as she fought to hold back her tears. She inhaled deeply, then raised her hand to the bandage on her neck. "I'm just glad he was with me. But Elinor, he—"

"I know," I interjected as I looked in the direction of the door. "He was still in that form when he brought you here." I turned to her. "What happened? All he said was that humans attacked you and that one man had injected you with poison. Father wanted to send the Guards after them, but all Cyrus would tell us was that he'd taken care of it."

"He killed them," Skye blurted, as if she couldn't bear to say the words. "He used magic I've never seen before, Elinor. And he had a power that I've never felt before either. It was . . ." She shook her head as she sighed. "It was dark, and . . . I just . . . if I hadn't already lost all feeling in my body, I would have been numb with shock." She took a deep breath. "But I knew he was still my Cyrus. It was just scary because somehow, he made one man turn to dust—just turn to dust! And I saw it, Elinor. I saw the excitement in Cyrus's eyes when it happened."

All we saw when he arrived with her was sheer panic. It wouldn't surprise me if the entire pack now knew what he felt for her. The situation had looked so dire, Nurse Hilary sent for Yathleen the elf immediately. The woman had arrived with a root that latched itself onto Skye's neck and sucked the poison from her system.

Though only semi-conscious, Skye cried and moaned in agony the entire time. Cyrus couldn't handle seeing Skye suffering so badly and had turned to my father for comfort.

"I get it. We were all shocked when we saw him. In fact, we all sensed him coming long before he arrived. He's strong

—stronger than any of us realized, but . . ." I grinned. "It's kind of cute how crazy he went over you, don't you think?"

I watched as she blushed, expecting her to tell me that Cyrus would do the same thing for anyone . . . but she didn't.

"We kissed," she blurted, and my eyes popped.

"Excuse me, what?" I asked as I scooted closer to her. "When did this happen? How? Why am I just hearing about it now?"

"We actually . . . um . . . he, um . . ." Her eyes drifted to the door, then she leaned forward. "He fed on me."

"Excuse me? He what?!" I yelled, and she slapped her hand over my mouth. I pulled her hand away. "Really?" I asked more quietly, and she nodded.

"So he took your virginity?" I asked in a rushed tone, needing to know all the details. For years, my two dearest friends had obvious feelings for each other—or obvious to me, at least—and finally, it looked like they'd stopped dancing around it.

"Goddess, no," she answered quickly, her cheeks now scarlet. "We just kissed, and he—" She closed her eyes. "He touched me, and that's all. He did something to me. I don't know how to explain it, but suddenly, I wanted him so badly I couldn't think of anything else. I would have had sex with him right there on the floor, but he said he wouldn't do that with me."

"On the floor?" I squealed, and we both erupted into laughter. "Oh my Goddess, you're both animals! I can't believe this. Finally, this is happening." She narrowed her eyes at me, and I nodded. "Oh yeah, I've known about the two of you for years. It's about damn time."

Skye smiled, apparently relieved that everything was

finally out in the open. "Oh, before I forget, I was telling Cyrus that I think it would be a great idea for him to teach the pups about all the different kinds of supernatural species there are, especially dark creatures. I mean, the children honestly receive very little education about such things, and Cyrus has been around. If they had a dark creature as their teacher, they'd understand that not all things labeled as dark are evil, you know?"

She gave me a very intense look, and for a moment, it confused me . . . until I realized what she was trying to say. I nodded my head in return. Even though the pack accepted him, I'd known for some time that Cyrus still sometimes felt like an outsider. If he had a job to do, he probably wouldn't feel the need to leave as often as he did.

"You're right. We keep the children close to home since they're so vulnerable at that age. But they learn little about the world outside of the pack. That needs to change."

"Exactly," she replied. Then she leaned back against the wall, her eyes seeming to grow tired.

"I'll talk to Father about it. But in the meantime, I think you should get some more rest. You just woke up, after all."

"I'm fine. After all, I've been asleep for two days. But before I forget, I wanted to ask, what happened a few nights ago when Connor howled a warning that you were in danger? I know you, so don't feed me the same crap he did, that he thought you had slipped off the cliff. You were out there meeting Will, weren't you?"

I turned away from her. I'd gone back to the cliff looking for Will after that night, but he didn't come back.

"Yes," I confirmed, eager to tell Skye about Will somehow wiping Connor's memory, when Cyrus entered the room.

"Um, but you need to rest. I'm okay," I quickly said as he returned to his seat by her side.

"What's wrong?" Cyrus probed as he handed Skye a cup of water.

"Nothing," I answered, standing up to leave. So far, Skye was the only one I'd told about Will. I wanted to tell Cyrus, but I had no idea how he'd react. "I'm just a little stressed out about the whole getting married thing. Elijah will return in three weeks, and we'll officially announce our engagement to the rest of the pack at that point. I'm just not sure how I feel about it."

Skye was still looking at me with concern. But since she knew my marriage to Elijah wasn't the only thing on my mind, she said nothing. She reached out her hand to me, and I quickly took it.

"I'm glad you're awake," I told her as I squeezed her hand. "I'll go talk to my father about your idea of letting Cyrus teach. I'll let you know what he says, okay?" They both nodded, and I turned and left.

"Hey," Cyrus called after me, and I glanced at him over my shoulder. "Are you sure you're okay?"

I nodded, my chest tightening. "Trust me, I'm fine."

4

ELINOR

If anyone were to walk by me now, they'd think I was crazy, given the way I was smiling. Skye and Cyrus were finally on the same page about their feelings for each other, and I couldn't be happier for both of them.

The way Skye smiled up at him filled me with happiness —something that had been definitely lacking in my life lately. I wasn't even mad that Skye hadn't told me about their encounter sooner. I was just thrilled it had happened—even if, like Will and me, they wouldn't be able to share their love for each other with the rest of the people in their lives.

Skye's mother might not mind having a demon for a son-in-law, but most of the pack definitely would. In the end, it came down to this: interspecies relationships were forbidden for werewolves. And while Skye was a werewolf, Cyrus wasn't.

Because we had predetermined mates, many wolves believed that being with anyone else besides your mate—even within our species—was taboo. We had to take so many factors into consideration . . . What happened if a wolf met her mate after having kids with another? Many times, the mate bond was so strong, two wolves would fall for each other immediately. But that wasn't a good thing if one wolf already had a family . . .

The mate bond was powerful, and when it worked, it really worked. The rejection rate between wolves was very, very low. But it happened. In those rare cases when a wolf rejected a mate, it could lead to the rejected wolf's death. The trauma of losing a true mate could leave a wolf shattered. I hadn't even known of any rejected wolves until I met Meeka at the Werewolf Guard examination. She'd said it had taken her years to recover.

Now, though, as someone who harbored feelings for someone who wasn't a wolf, I felt torn. At least Skye and Cyrus had a tiny chance of being together, considering our pack had accepted Cyrus long ago. But Will and I . . . we could never be. Even simply being friends was dangerous.

If I were to meet my mate, whatever there was between Will and me would end. We'd made no grand declarations to each other. The chaos of our friendship being discovered was what I feared the most. My mind instantly took me back to that night at the cliff and the smile on my face faltered. If Will hadn't done whatever magic he did to Connor, my father would have learned the truth. And he'd have ordered the Guards to hunt Will down and kill him.

I wasn't sure what kind of reaction Will's kind would have. Would they have killed him for befriending a wolf, or would they have been satisfied with just killing me? And if my father had orchestrated Will's death, would his kind have retaliated?

I pressed my fingers into my eyes. This shouldn't be so

hard. I had to end things with him—the risk was just too great. Even so, my chest tightened at the thought of losing him.

I sighed as my hand fell to my side.

Is he even worrying about this the way I am?

I'd been keeping a close eye on Connor, watching him to see if his memory of that night would return. It had been days, but so far, the events of that night seemed forgotten.

I needed to put my foot down and find out who Will truly was. Every time I thought it was okay to get comfortable with him, something new happened that showed me I knew absolutely nothing about him.

The fact that he had a beating heart and somehow alternated between being cold to the touch, as vampires should be, and then warm like a human was another thing I needed more details about. For a time, I'd even wondered if he was truly a vampire. Of course, those doubts had been washed away. Nevertheless, I needed to figure him out once and for all. Was he a regular vampire or a more powerful one? And did all vampires have such strength and skill? If they did, we were in trouble.

"Elinor!"

I froze, then looked up and realized I was already back to my house. I'd been too deep in thought to notice. When I looked to my left, I saw Nurse Hilary and Ione walking towards me. Ione's blue eyes shone brightly as she waved to me.

"Hey, Ione." I waved back at her and walked over to meet them. "Hi, Nurse Hilary. Did you hear? Skye is awake!"

Hilary nodded as her blond hair, so much like her daughter's, danced around her. "I did. It's wonderful news. But there is something Ione and I need to do before I head over to Skye's place."

Ione's smile stretched even further. "I'm remembering my visions now, Elinor. Just bits and pieces, but still, I can remember them."

"Really?" I asked, sharing her excitement. Ione was an Enchanted, and a major part of her abilities included seeing visions from time to time. Her inability to remember her visions had been very frustrating for her . . . until now.

She had one of her visions in my presence not long ago. She warned me to be careful on the night of a full moon. I didn't understand what she was talking about when she had the vision, so I'd nearly forgotten about it. At only fourteen years old, Ione had a lot to learn in order to become a powerful Enchanted, but she was well on her way.

I thought back to her warning. A vampire almost killed me on a night with a full moon . . . but that was also the night I'd met Will. Had Ione seen our meeting? And if so, what else had she seen?

"That's great," I said, placing my hand on her shoulder.

"That's why we need to see your father," Hilary interjected, and the pleasant smile vanished from her face. She looked down at Ione. The corners of Ione's mouth drew downward into an expression of profound sadness and regret.

"What's wrong?" I asked, looking from one to the other. "Did something happen?"

Ione nodded. "It did. But I saw it too late." She swallowed. "I had a vision of Keith." My eyes widened at the mention of the local boy who was murdered. "I saw the moment of his death on the night of the festival. Like I said, I only recall bits and pieces, but I remember enough that I think it might help the Alpha find whoever's behind it."

We all started walking towards the house. I felt both excited and relieved that we might finally have a lead on who —or what—had killed one of our own. "What did you see?"

"I-I saw parts of the festival, people drinking and all. I saw Keith talking to several pack members and even Cyrus. But then things got foggy." Ione paused at the door, and Hilary and I stopped with her. "Then my vision switched to viewing everything through Keith's eyes. He couldn't see who attacked him, so I couldn't either. But I heard hissing."

"Hissing?" I repeated. I looked at Hilary, and she nodded. "So, you're thinking vampire even though there were no bite marks on the body?"

She nodded again. "I know we had almost ruled out vampires, but it is possible. Not all vampires are alike. Of course, it could also have been any other creature we know that hisses."

"This will help, won't it?" Ione asked me, hope shining in her eyes. I knew she must be relieved to finally be able to use her Enchanted abilities to help the pack.

"It definitely will. Now we can narrow down the search for whoever killed him." I opened the door for them and stepped to the side as they entered the house.

"I mean, there aren't many creatures that hiss," Hilary added. "I can't help thinking it was a vampire. After all, we really know so little about them or the abilities they have. They might have developed an alternative way of feeding."

Will.

"My guess is it was a Skin. A Bleeder wouldn't have been

able to stop himself from doing more damage," Hilary continued. But I was lost in thought.

Hilary was right. I'd just learned that vampires had all kinds of abilities we weren't aware of. If Will could have a beating heart, was it so crazy to think that his kind might be capable of feeding without biting?

My heart throbbed in my chest. Will might know something about what had happened to Keith and the other victims. He'd been at the festival, after all. Maybe he saw something? And I had to consider . . . I had no idea what he did before I saw him that night—or afterward, for that matter.

Still, there were other Skins at the festival, too. Maybe they were responsible? This was giving me a headache.

"Elinor, are you okay?" Hilary looked at me with pursed lips, as if she was performing a mental medical assessment of my condition.

"Mm? Oh yes," I rubbed at my temple. "Just thinking about everything, that's all."

She nodded. "It's a lot to take in."

And she didn't even know about the other deaths yet. My father had told me what was really going on, about the other victims from other species and other towns. Few people knew how bad it really was.

Still, it was great that Ione could remember that vision now. My father would leave in a few days to meet up with the leaders of the other species that had lost people to this new threat. Surely this news could help in some capacity.

"Well, my father should be in his office," I answered. As Hilary walked away, Ione remained by my side.

"I remember the vision I had of you," she blurted out. I

frowned, confused for a moment before I realized what she was speaking of. "I saw you fighting a Bleeder. It attacked you. If only I had been stronger or had remembered my vision back then, I would have been able to help. I'm sorry, Elinor. Because of me, you almost died."

I placed my hand on her shoulder and turned her to face me, my green eyes boring into her blue ones. "Please don't think like that. I didn't almost die because of you. I almost died because I was foolish enough to run into the forest during a full moon. I don't want you to blame yourself, okay? You're not some tool—you're just a girl trying to learn some control over her gifts. I was powerful enough that night to beat those Skins, and you're getting better at remembering your visions. You're improving at your own speed and with your own effort—that's what matters. Okay?"

"Are you sure?" she asked. I released her shoulder as I stood up straight. The way she was looking at me reminded me so much of how I used to look at my father. I used to trust his words so much.

"I'm sure," I told her. "I'm happy you're getting stronger. You're one of the most important members of our pack, Ione."

Her eyes lit up with joy. "Do you really mean that?"

"Of course. No one else has such a cool gift. By the way, what about your nightmares? Have they stopped, or are you remembering them now as well?"

She shook her head. "No, those are still a mystery. But don't worry, I'll start remembering those soon, too, I hope. Then I'll know why I keep having them."

"Good." I ruffled her hair and earned myself a semi-disgusted look, though she was still smiling. "Now go do your thing, Enchanted." I winked at her and watched as she climbed the stairs with her mother to the second floor of the house.

I sighed once they were out of my sight. Deep down, I was worried—worried that Will might have been the one who killed Keith.

Could it have been him? And if it was, what was I going to do?

Skye

I watched Cyrus as he gazed out my window. It was almost time for bed, and other than helping my mother make dinner, he hadn't left my side. Nurse Hilary had stopped by to remove the bandage on my neck, and he stayed the entire time as my silent guardian. My mother told me he was there the full two days I slept as well.

I smiled as my heart swelled with gratitude for this man. For the second time, he'd saved my life.

I gazed at him standing there so calmly and then thought of the raging beast I had seen him become.

"Cyrus?" I called, and he turned around instantly. "Are you okay?" He walked over to me and sat on the bed beside me. "Hilary said I can get up and move around tomorrow."

"Yeah, I heard. That's good news. I know you hate being stuck in bed."

You know me too well.

"Yeah . . . Cyrus, can I talk to you about something?" I asked. He exhaled heavily, as if he had been waiting for me to say something. "In the alley . . . what happened to you? What kind of power was that?"

He turned to the window once more but didn't answer right away. Then he combed his hair back and looked back at me. He closed his eyes briefly. "Black magic," he whispered. "Magic I inherited from my father." He picked up my hand. "Were you . . . afraid of me?"

I shook my head immediately. "No, no, of course not. I mean, you looked . . . scary, but I knew it was you. You wouldn't hurt me. I just . . ." I sighed. "We've never been in a situation like that before, so of course I'd never seen that side of you. But now that I have, I can't help wondering what else there is that I don't know about you. We grew up together, and yet you're still such a mystery sometimes."

"Come on," he chuckled, his eyes turning to slits as he smiled. "You know me. There's not much more to know."

I didn't smile back, and soon his smile died. And though he was trying to hide it, I could see the truth in his eyes— there were a *lot* of things I didn't know about Cyrus.

"You know you can tell me anything, right?" I asked, and he frowned. I glimpsed a look of worry on his face before he turned away. "Right?" I repeated.

"I know," he answered. And while I waited for him to say more, he didn't.

Sighing, I rubbed at my temple. "I know you hide a lot of your true nature from us—from me. What you did the other day made that clear."

"I have to," he groaned. I took his hand, hoping he'd realize he could trust me with anything. "As much as I hate it, the fact is that I'm the son of the Demon King and a Sin. I can't be around you and Elinor or the pack without holding back my true nature. I've worked too hard to have the control that I do, and I can't be careless with that side of myself."

"A little too much control, if you ask me," I grumbled, and he chuckled.

"Sure, maybe a little too much, but you've been helping me with that." A mischievous smile curved the corner of his lips, and my stomach clenched at the memory of what we did —of our kiss. "We haven't talked about what happened."

"We don't need to," I told him as he reached up and cupped my cheek. "If I can help you, I will, always. But—" His brow arched at that. "Do you regret it? Feeding on me, I mean. Or our kiss?"

He ran his thumb under my lip as he squeezed my hand. "I don't regret a single thing we did. I care about you, Skye. A lot. And what happened between us was something I had thought about many, many times." His nostrils flared at that moment, and I looked away in embarrassment. He leaned forward and pressed his cheek to mine, his breath blowing hot against my ear. "Try not to get excited, Skye, or I won't be able to stop myself. And you need to rest."

He moved so quickly I didn't have time to prepare myself before he turned my head and pressed his lips to mine. This kiss wasn't gentle but filled with passion, and he held me by my neck to keep me close. I threw my arms over his shoulder as our kiss became more heated, but I hoped he could feel more than just my passion. I wanted him to feel my emotions, my gratitude for having him in my life. He tore himself away from me, and I held my breath as I saw his eyes go dark. They roamed over my face and down my body before he suddenly closed them and got up.

"Rest," he told me, his voice deeper than usual.

"Wait," I said as I held his hand. He glanced down at me, but he had already turned the rest of his body toward the door, as if he couldn't fully face me. "Stay," I whispered. "Just until I fall asleep. Please."

He slowly turned back to me, his black eyes gradually returning to their normal color, and I scooted over on my bed to make room for him to lie down. After I was snuggled in his arms with my head on his chest, I wondered how he could ever think he'd scare me. I was a werewolf with above-average strength and skills, but I always felt a heightened sense of security with him around.

"What do you think about Keith's death?" I asked after a few moments of silence. If humans could randomly attack me, an adult werewolf, maybe those same men were responsible for Keith's death too . . . although that wouldn't explain how his blood had been completely drained. "Do you think the men who attacked me could have had something to do with it?"

Cyrus hummed, the sound calming, and I closed my eyes. "I doubt that. It's possible, of course—" He cleared his throat. "But I doubt it." He rested his chin on the top of my head. "I'm just really curious to know what could have drained him of his blood without leaving any sort of mark. I don't know of an earthly creature that can do that."

"Maybe you should apply to become a Guard with all these kills you have," I joked, and his chest shook as he laughed.

"A demon in the Werewolf Guard? I can definitely see that happening." He kissed the top of my head. "As long as you and Elinor are safe, no one has to see the side of me you saw in the market. Go to sleep, Skye."

My eyes were tired, and I fell asleep right away knowing that no harm would come to me as long as Cyrus was around. I knew his mother wanted him to return to the Underworld, but I wouldn't let him go so easily.

5

WILL

The wind howling outside sounded like the wailing of a woman in mourning. A sudden snowstorm appeared a few hours ago, but it wasn't all that surprising, given the change in temperature from a few days earlier.

With my heart currently beating and my skin warm, I could appreciate the heat from the fire I lit in the fireplace. The first day I arrived here, I was both confused and overjoyed to find a chimney in a vampire's house. I later found out the owners added it just weeks after my visit to this coven was confirmed, even though I'd shown up early.

I crossed my legs as I gazed into the fire, my eyes expertly tracking the flames as they danced. I had secretly dreaded the thought of coming to this coven, but if I hadn't come, I never would have met her.

Elinor.

I exhaled heavily as I clenched my fists. I had finally gotten the chance to taste her, to feel her . . . until that damn wolf interrupted us. As I recalled the way Elinor's skin felt under my fingers, I closed my eyes. I swallowed as I thought about how her lips touched mine.

My fangs ached with need—a need to taste more than just her lips.

Shaking my head, I slowly opened my eyes. I took a deep breath, inhaling the scent of the burning wood to rid myself of my thirst for her. I thought about the problems it would cause, not only with her kind but with mine as well if anyone ever discovered our relationship. But even that thought hadn't stopped me from seeing her.

Over the past few weeks, my cravings for her had grown even stronger. And though I recognized that a romantic relationship between us was impossible—she was the daughter of the Alpha and I a high-ranked vampire among my kind—I just couldn't stay away from her.

I was not sure if knowledge of my noble birth would make her think of me any differently. Most people shunned vampires, considering us all to be monsters. And sure, when we first met, Elinor probably saw me that way, too—though she hadn't acted like it.

The evening we met, I saw her as nothing but potential food—if I had been hungry, that was. But the way she had reacted to me was unusual. Despite recognizing exactly what I was, she hadn't been afraid. She'd charmed me from the beginning.

I shook my head as I smiled, the memory of me saving her from a newly-born Bleeder resurfacing in my mind. It had been that night that I realized just how different she was. Though she was young, she had spirit and not just strength.

"Sir Hunter?"

I looked over my shoulder to find a human servant standing by the door. "Yes, Violet? Come forward."

She smiled warmly as she entered the room and held out a letter to me, bowing slightly. "For you, sir."

"Thank you," I replied, watching as she walked away.

That had been another surprise—and a refreshing one— at this property. It was unusual to see human servants who were actually servants and not slaves—or worse. Of course, in the basement, there were various supernaturals who'd been caught to be used as a food source for this coven, but I avoided that part of the estate. I was a vampire, yes, but an old one—an *ancient* one. I'd outgrown the cruelty of my kind long ago.

I opened the letter, knowing full well who it was from. I read it slowly, my irritation and anger increasing as I scanned through it. It contained certain directives that I planned to fully ignore.

Leave it up to my mother to spoil my moment of peace, even from a distance.

Ripping up the letter, I stood up and threw it into the fire. Just then, I heard footsteps approaching.

"Who was that letter from?" a soft voice asked. But I simply stood there, my eyes glued to the flames as they consumed the parchment. "Will?"

"No one, Vivian. It's none of your concern." I turned to face the attractive woman standing by the door, whose crimson hair cascading down to her ankles matched her blood-red eyes. She frowned at my sharp response.

"Fine, then." Sighing, she walked forward. "Are you okay, Will? I've been very worried about you. My father did his best to make our coven as comfortable for you as possible during your stay, but you're always out somewhere. And when you're here, you seem distant and distracted."

"We've never been close, Vivian, so how can I seem more distant? I'm only here because my mother requested that I stay with you while your father handles business out of the country. But you and I both know you don't need the protection. The locals have no clue there's a vampire coven living right under their noses."

"We've never been close, but that's just one more reason we invited you here—so maybe we could be. And you're right, I don't need protection. The supernaturals don't know about us because we live peacefully with them. We only take what we need, as Father commands." Her eyes drifted to the fireplace, then she tilted her head, seeming to be listening to something. "Hearing that sound never gets old," she chuckled. "You're a vampire with a heartbeat, Will. You're lucky you can enjoy life more than the rest of us."

"You're a hundred years old, Vivian. Your ancestors weren't even alive when I started making full use of my gifts," I told her, and she arched her brow. *Damn.* Not that I disliked her, but there'd always been something about Vivian that rubbed me the wrong way. I could see a savagery behind her eyes that her father had to constantly keep in check. Sighing, I turned to the fire and clapped my hands, the air movement from the action causing the fire to go out in the blink of an eye. "Do you need help with anything right now?"

"No," she answered. "Are you leaving?"

I nodded as I stepped around her. "I am, though I won't be out long."

Her fingers wrapped around my elbow. "Many vampires might see you as an outcast because of your gift, but I don't see it that way. We're family, Will. If there is ever anything bothering you, you can talk to me. Why have you been going out so much? Are you going to hunt? We have more than enough food here for you if you want it."

"I'll be back soon, Vivian." I covered her hand with mine. "Okay?"

She pulled her hand away as her red eyes flashed. "Okay, I get it. When are you leaving?"

I turned away, leaving her standing there. If it were up to me, I would never have come here at all, so her sudden attitude change didn't faze me. There were very few vampires I got along with, and it had been that way since I'd first changed. Thankfully, I was not the savage beast I once was, and the old stories about me had mostly faded from memory.

Now my only interest was a spirited she-wolf who'd inconveniently wormed her way into my heart.

"I have a few things to take care of first. I won't be leaving for a while."

Elinor

I waited until the snowstorm raging outside let up before venturing into the forest. Now that my father had left to meet with the other supernatural leaders, I could finally move more freely as well.

I'd gone into the forest twice, hoping to see Will after our last meeting, but both times he was nowhere to be found. And escaping into the woods to search for him was becoming difficult—the guards patrolling our territory almost caught me both times. What was more frustrating, however, was that ever since Connor had claimed I came close to falling off that cliff, my father had been keeping a very close eye on me.

As I made my way through the snow-covered forest, I wondered if he had believed I'd try to kill myself or some madness of the sort. Rolling my eyes, I stepped over an old, rotten tree trunk. I could make out the sound of the water below the cliff, but I remained within the forest area, just in case the cliff was being watched. But so far, I hadn't sensed or smelled another wolf.

Did Father really think I'd kill myself?

"I might hate the idea of marrying Elijah, but I'm not about to end it all over that," I mumbled to myself.

"That's good to know," a voice said from behind me. I spun around to find Will casually leaning against a tree, his all-black attire contrasting with our snow-covered surroundings. I hadn't even heard him approach—or smelled him, for that matter. Had I been too deep in thought to notice? I didn't know. But I needed to be more careful in the future.

I heard it immediately—his beating heart—and sighed. Whenever he appeared like this, with a beating heart and warm skin, his vampire scent seemed to vanish.

"Where have you been?" I blurted out, and his lips curved with a smile.

"You missed me?" he asked as he pushed himself off the tree and walked over to me.

The memory of him above me in the cold grass not so long ago resurfaced, and my breath caught in my throat. But I wasn't about to let him know that. So I rolled my eyes and turned away. "I just have a few questions I need answered."

I listened to the sound of his footsteps behind me as I walked close to the tree line near the cliff. I needed to know what he did to Connor the other day. But more importantly, I needed to know if vampires were involved with Keith's death or the others'.

Yet how could I go about asking him that without sounding like I was accusing him, too? Or making him feel like I was judging his kind? While vampires were undoubtedly savage hunters, particularly the Bleeders, they weren't the only supernaturals capable of murder.

I turned around. "Listen, I want you to—"

His lips were on mine before I knew what was happening, and my mind went blank for a moment. All the questions I wanted to ask disappeared when I felt his hands rest on my hips. He pulled me closer to him, and I sighed at the warmth of his embrace. My arms acted on their own, throwing themselves over his shoulders as I dove my fingers into his hair.

His hair was like silk, and his lips tasted divine. His body felt like a mountain of muscles.

Then I had a sudden thought that had me pulling myself out of his arms. If he had controlled Connor with his mind, was there a chance he was doing the same thing to me? Compulsion.

"Didn't your mother ever teach you not to kiss women without asking?"

He shrugged. "I've seen her kiss many women without permission, then rip out their throats, so I guess my mother hasn't exactly been the best role model for manners." My eyes widened for a moment, and he chuckled. "I missed you too, Little Wolf, but I was . . . occupied."

"That wasn't funny," I grumbled.

He shrugged. "Wasn't there something you wanted to ask me?"

I was all too happy to change the subject. "What did you do to Connor that night? You spoke to him and suddenly, he thought I had almost fallen over the cliff instead of remembering what had really happened. What did you do?"

"Right," he drawled. "Of course, you'd be curious about that. I compelled him to forget what he saw, that's all." He looked towards the cliff behind me. "Not all vampires are capable of compulsion. It takes decades of practice."

"Decades?" I asked, and his eyes drifted back to mine.

He tilted his head to the side, his black hair almost blending into the darkness behind him. "Yes, decades. I'm centuries old, Elinor. I was alive when this little town was still just a vast forest. Does that bother you?"

"Doesn't it bother you? I'm just a baby to you," I answered, shaking my head and trying not to grin. "Shame on you."

His face twisted with disgust. "Don't make this weird."

I chuckled at his discomfort, happy that I'd finally found something that truly irritated him. "It's hard to imagine what it'd be like to have lived so long," I said truthfully as he reached out and took a lock of my hair between his fingers. I quickly slapped his hand. "No touching."

"I thought you liked it when I touched you, Elinor. You make the most adorable sounds." He chuckled as he walked around me, circling me once before stopping in front of me. He leaned forward to kiss me again, but this time I was prepared. I pulled away, causing his lips to only brush against mine. But somehow, even that slight touch had my body heating.

I quickly changed the subject again, telling him about the string of murders in the area. "Anyway, the boy from my pack who was killed? He wasn't the first," I said. "There were other supernaturals from other towns who were murdered the same way. But so far, the Werewolf Guards haven't been able to find out anything. Is there any chance you might know something about what's going on?"

"Why would I know about that?" His eyes narrowed, and I could see the walls going up behind his eyes. A humorless chuckle left his lips. "You think I had something to do with it, don't you?"

I shook my head. "No. But all the victims had their blood drained, and there was no mark. That's not normal, Will. I was only asking if you knew or had heard anything that could help me. Someone, or something, killed a boy from my pack. I'm only trying to find out who did it."

"You're not a Guard," he argued, and I clenched my fists. His words stung more than he'd ever know.

"Wow, really, I didn't know that. Thanks for pointing that out." I took a deep breath. "What I'm trying to say, Will, is that Keith won't be the last victim. People are getting killed."

He brushed his knuckles against his chin, and his tongue darted out to wet his lips. "I understand, Elinor, and I can see why you might suspect a vampire if people are turning up drained of their blood. The thing is—" He held a finger up. "Vampires don't do that often unless they are a newborn. We have the same organs that you do, which means our stomachs can't hold all that blood. So when you find a drained body, you know a very young vampire who lacks control over their bloodlust is behind it."

"And the lack of bite marks? Can a vampire do that?"

He looked thoughtful for a moment before shaking his head. "No, a vampire must bite their victim. We can heal the wounds of whoever we bite, but that doesn't work once a person is dead and drained of their blood. A vampire isn't the one doing this."

I closed my eyes, pressing the pads of my fingers against them. "Okay then. My pack's Enchanted had a vision of Keith the night he died." My hand fell away from my face. "She heard hissing."

Will's blue eyes suddenly changed to red as he reached out and grabbed my arm firmly. I held my hand out to push against his chest, but he turned his back to me. I blinked with confusion. "Come out," he hissed into the darkness. "Now."

I peeped out from behind him and saw a towering form materializing out of thin air. My eyes widened as I stared at Cyrus in his demon form. The black marks on his body were drifting as his bright eyes slid from Will to me and then back.

"Cyrus?" I stepped out from behind Will, but he quickly grabbed my hand.

"Do you know this demon, Elinor?" he asked, and Cyrus's eyes changed to red.

"You have two seconds to step away from her," Cyrus growled, and I sighed as my shoulders slumped.

Here we go again.

6

ELINOR

*N*ot wanting to see a repeat of the fight that had happened between Will and Connor, I quickly stepped in front of Will, my feet crunching in the snow. "Cyrus, I know him. He won't hurt me. And I'd prefer it if the two of you could knock your testosterone levels down a notch and just chill for a minute while I explain."

Cyrus shook his head. "I didn't think you'd be this foolish, Elinor." My eyes widened at that, his words cutting me deep. "He's a vampire, a Skin. He's not your friend. How did the two of you even meet?"

Gritting my teeth, I stepped forward, my eyes narrowing. "I don't know, Cyrus. Maybe we met the same way Skye met you. You're the last person who should judge my friendship with Will. While I might be foolish, you're being a hypocrite. Which do you think is worse?"

I hated this. It was the first time Cyrus and I had ever argued. And I was having trouble taking him all in. His form seemed much bigger than the last time I'd seen him. And his eyes were red instead of the black they used to be. He was getting stronger.

His body burst into black smoke. By the time the smoke faded, he had returned to his human form. "I didn't mean to offend you, Elinor. I just . . . you had me worried for a minute there." He looked at Will over my shoulder, and I watched as his nostrils twitched. "Why don't you have the same pungent scent that other vampires do?"

I made a face. "You don't have to say it like that," I mumbled under my breath as I turned to look at Will.

Will's eyes drifted to me for a moment before he moved his cloak forward to shield his body. "I just don't. If I knew, I'd tell you," he answered.

Cyrus made a sound in the back of his throat. "That's doubtful." His eyes shot to Will's chest. "You have a heartbeat!" He stepped forward and then stopped, looking between me and Will. "How is that even possible?"

Will didn't answer right away, and it left me wondering what he was thinking. I squinted, noticing the way his jaw clenched. Sure, Cyrus's interruption upset me, too. But it seemed as if something else entirely was angering Will.

"Some vampires have special gifts," he answered. "My gift is a beating heart."

"Then you're not a vampire, right?" Cyrus said, and I smacked his arm. "What? He's a vampire with a beating heart. But not having a beating heart is exactly what makes a vampire a *vampire*, right?" Cyrus posed the question to me, as if he didn't trust Will to answer honestly.

"Is this really necessary, Cyrus? Yes, he's a vampire. End of story. Do you want to see his fangs? Or better still, why don't you show him your demon eyes? You know, since you're a demon on wolf territory. It's better to confirm what we all are and what we're not, right?"

"I think it's time for me to take my leave," Will said as he stepped forward. "It seems like you two have a lot to talk about. But in the meantime, I'll look into what you asked me about." He lifted a hand and ran his knuckles across my cheek. Knowing Cyrus was watching behind me had me blushing in embarrassment. Will's lips curved ever so slightly. "I'll see you soon, Little Wolf."

Then, right before my eyes, he vanished. A few strands of my hair blew in the wind created by his little disappearing act. Then I turned to Cyrus and growled, "So you're an asshole now, is that it? You get a new demon form and turn into an asshole? You didn't have to be rude."

"I asked a valid question," he said, shrugging.

"So I'd be in the right if I kicked your ass right now? Because I was in the middle of getting information about Keith's death."

He snorted, shaking his head. "Yeah, that's not what I saw." He sighed, then blinked three times and crossed his arms over his chest. Confused, I looked him up and down until I realized he was waiting for me to explain.

"I'm waiting."

"I know," I growled as I walked past him.

"Does Skye know about this?" he asked as we ambled through the woods, surrounded by the soothing sounds of nocturnal creatures calling to each other.

"Yes." I lifted my skirt and bundled it in my hand to avoid it getting dirty. "I asked her not to tell you because I knew you'd freak out . . . even though you, of all people, should understand."

"Can you blame me?" he asked. "Yeah, I get it. I'm a demon and he's a vampire, and in terms of danger, there isn't a big difference between us. But honestly, that's exactly what concerns me. And I sure as hell would have preferred it if you'd told me he existed before I discovered you just inches away from a strange vampire in the dark of night in the middle of the forest. Especially after a vampire almost killed you not so long ago."

I sighed. "Yeah, I get it. Sorry. But you don't have to worry about me. Like you, he's different from the rest of his kind."

"Yeah, his heartbeat confirmed that much," he grumbled as we stopped walking a mile from Skye's house. "So, how did you two meet?"

I took a deep breath, then told him all about the evening I'd met Will. At the time, he'd been nothing but a vampire passing by, but afterward, he saved me in the woods when I was attacked by Bleeders.

I told Cyrus about all the times we met up after that, and what happened at the cliff with Connor. As I spoke, Cyrus remained silent.

After I finished speaking, he just looked at me, not saying a single word. I wasn't bothered by that, though. Cyrus wasn't normally chatty. However, after five minutes had passed, I started to get a little worried. "Cyrus?"

"We should hurry back," he said in response.

But I stopped and took his arm. He turned to face me, inhaling deeply.

I couldn't decipher the look in his eyes. Was there disappointment there? "Say something, please. You always know what to say, Cyrus, and I value your opinion. I know this is a lot to take in. And I realize that getting close to Will, especially in the beginning, was foolish. But it just happened."

Cyrus shook his head. "I want to tell you to stay away from him, that he's dangerous . . . But you were right—I don't have the right to say that. Not when I'm here, with you and Skye and your pack, not when I'm in lo—" He looked away quickly as he bit down on his lip, and my eyes widened at what he almost said.

"I know," I told him, and his cheeks turned red. "I already know."

"Anyway . . ." He turned away as we continued walking, and I watched as small snowflakes fell onto his cloak. "You all accepted me as a demon, so it's not my place to say this, but . . . they'll never accept Will. Honestly, I just hope you know what you're doing."

"But what if I don't?" I said more to myself than him.

He said nothing in response as he took my hand and squeezed it. "Just be careful, okay? Just because he has a beating heart doesn't mean he wouldn't suck you dry if he got thirsty enough."

Alpha Grayson

I watched the leader of the witches as she conversed with the leader of the elves and found it curious that they both had paper white hair. I could hear their conversation clearly as they spoke among themselves about the meeting we'd just had.

As expected, there was little to no information about who

had killed Keith and the others. Ione's vision had proved useful, though. The Werewolf Council sent an Enchanted to meet with her in hopes she'd somehow be able to get more information from the vision.

Enchanteds—said to be descendants of our Goddess—had always been a mystery to me. Elinor's bright eyes flashed in my mind, and I thought about the myth surrounding wolves with pure white fur like hers. At least the information about Enchanteds being the descendants of the Goddess was actually factual and not just a bedtime story for pups. But ever since Elinor had first transformed, I knew I'd have to protect her at all costs. Now, we barely spoke to each other, and I had no one to blame but myself.

"Thank you for the information you provided, Alpha Grayson." Faelen—the Enchanted sent by the Werewolf Council—sat down beside me as she, too, observed the witch and elf. She chuckled as she ran a hand down the thick white braid that pooled in her lap. "I guess having white hair isn't that unique, huh?"

"For Enchanteds, it is," I told her.

She turned to face me, her striking blue eyes blinking slowly. "Thank you for your help with this hunt. It would seem you have a promising Enchanted amongst your pack."

"She's still learning, but I know one day when she becomes as powerful as you are, she'll be walking around with white hair like an elf, too."

She chuckled. "Hey, don't tease. All elves have white hair, but for an Enchanted, it's a sign of our strength." A smug smile appeared on her lips. "Besides, I quite like my white hair."

"Of course," I replied, and we sat in silence for a moment.

Faelen was second in line to become a Grand Elder. Much like witches who had coven leaders and a Grand Witch, Enchanteds had a Grand Elder. The Grand Elder was a powerful Enchanted with a strong connection to the Goddess. Because of that connection, she was able to cast certain spells—much like a witch could. Although they were werewolves, Enchanteds couldn't transform, and for that reason, they had their own governing council.

If you asked me, Enchanteds probably should have been in charge of all werewolves. After all, they were the ones with a direct link to our Goddess. But other werewolves argued we should choose our leaders from the strongest among us, and werewolves who couldn't transform didn't stand a chance of competing in brute physical strength. I thought it probably had more to do with many of the males not wanting to answer to female leaders, but that was difficult to prove.

"How's your daughter?" Faelen asked as she turned to me. "Is it true what they say about her?"

I didn't answer right away, but I knew there was no point in trying to hide the truth. After Elinor took part in the Werewolf Guard examination, news of the existence of a white wolf spread throughout the packs like wildfire.

"Yes," I told her, and her eyes glimmered with curiosity.

"Your daughter is a special girl, indeed," she murmured under her breath. "Keep her close."

"So, I guess you believe the stories? She's my daughter, and although she's incredibly stubborn, I can attest that she's just a girl—a normal girl."

She smoothed her hand down her light purple dress, and her face grew serious. "Don't you? Believe the stories, I mean? I do, regardless of whether you do. I believe wolves with white coats are descendants of the first wolf created by the Goddess."

"She's a normal girl," I repeated, but Faelen shook her head.

"Have you ever allowed an experienced Enchanted to test her blood?" When I continued to stare at her, she elaborated. "I'm guessing that's a no. An Enchanted's blood contains divinity. The stronger the divinity, the stronger the connection to the Goddess. There are spells that can detect it."

"I didn't know that," I told her, but deep down, I knew I'd never subject Elinor to testing. I doubted she'd even allow it.

After everything I'd put her through, she'd probably fight me on anything I said. I was an Alpha—a leader—and a damn good one. But waging a war against my own daughter was getting tiring. One day, she'd realize that everything I did was for her own good.

And what if an Enchanted performed this test and results showed she actually did have divinity? How in the world would I protect her? She would be hunted for far more than just her hand in marriage.

Faelen placed her hand over mine. "I know what you're thinking, and you're right to worry. That is why I insist you do the test and get in front of this. There are many ways to test her blood without her knowing, and all we'd need is a drop." She removed her hand. "If it turns out she has divinity as well as the ability to shift, she'll be sought after for many reasons, both good and bad. And this unknown predator we've been discussing will be the least of your problems."

"The Council will try to take her," I said under my breath,

low enough so only she would hear, just in case our conversation was being overheard.

She nodded. "A werewolf with both divinity and the ability to shift would make history. The Council will want her close to watch her. She might develop abilities much like an Enchanted, perhaps even stronger." Then Faelen's eyes grew bitter. "Of course, they'll want to control her, the same way they control us Enchanteds."

I clenched my fists. As much as I'd rather forget this conversation ever happened, I couldn't help agreeing with Faelen that it was better for us to know for certain. I couldn't focus on that right now, though. The threat against my pack was growing, and I had to handle the problem before someone else got hurt. So many members of my pack were at that festival that night, including my daughter.

My clenched fists relaxed as a thought occurred to me. "It seems like the killer is moving in a straight line from one town to the next. Maybe we should start watching the next town a few miles away from mine in case they get hit next."

She looked thoughtful for a moment. "You're right. I hadn't noticed the pattern because we've all been so focused on figuring out who or what kind of creature it could be. I'll speak to the Council and have—"

"No," I cut her off. "There are no packs in or near that town, and it's a small one, so the number of Guards we'd need is minimal. We don't know what this thing is. We're not even sure if it's intelligent or just acting on instincts. We can't suddenly have Guards swarming the town." The wheels in my mind started to turn as I leaned forward, my eyes glued to the witch and elf as they slowly walked away. "To avoid suspicion, we should ask a few witches to go to the town, just to keep an eye on things. They could have a portal on standby if they discover who is doing this." *Yes, this could work.*

Faelen stood, and I followed suit. She smiled. "And Guards could be kept on standby elsewhere, ready to be teleported in at a moment's notice. It's a good plan, Grayson. The sooner we find this creature, the sooner we'll be able to confer about other matters."

"What other matters?" I inquired. The hesitation on her face as she looked around us was a bright red flag. Something else was definitely going on here.

"People have been disappearing," she said, low enough for only me to hear. "From all species and long before we found the first drained body. The disappearances have been growing in number recently. We have to do something about it."

"What disappearances? If people from all different species have been vanishing without a trace, why weren't the Guards made aware of it?"

"We needed to avoid panic at all costs. Because once again, we have no leads. A Council representative attended a meeting for leaders of all the species. But nobody had any answers. Now, we're finding bodies. Is it the same killer? We don't know, but we have to find out before more people go missing."

"How bad are we talking?" I asked, and she sighed heavily.

"More than two thousand supernaturals are missing at the moment. Reports keep coming in from all across the country. There are sixty-eight reported missing from this region alone."

I thought of Elinor and my pack, of my wife and son, and

of the people I held dear. My instinct as an Alpha to protect my people kicked in, and I felt a great need to return home immediately.

Elves, witches, centaurs, satyrs, humans, shifters, and naiads that lived within the forests—they were all in danger . . . and they didn't know it. Peace between the species had always been tenuous, but at times like this, we all had to put our differences aside for the common good.

A thought occurred to me, causing an unsettling feeling to rise in my chest. "What if both cases aren't the same?"

7

ELINOR

The snow was finally melting as the sun beamed down on the earth. For three days, a strong blizzard had trapped us all indoors.

As much as I had enjoyed the sound of the howling winds outside, I worried about my father. I mean, he was an Alpha—I was sure he could survive any snowstorm he got caught in, but despite our strained relationship at the moment, I'd hate for anything bad to happen to him.

There was one good thing about the storm. Since the blizzard forced humans and supernaturals alike indoors, whoever had killed Keith wouldn't be able to do any more hunting.

Beside me, Skye sighed as she lifted her head upward, soaking up the rays of sun beaming down on us. She stretched out her legs and crossed them at the ankles before resting her head against the tree trunk behind her.

"Are you comfortable enough?" I asked, chuckling as she bobbed her head.

"Oh yes. You know how I hate being trapped inside. That storm was a pain in the ass."

"Three days trapped inside with Cyrus couldn't have been that bad," I said.

She closed her eyes, crossed her arms, and began shuffling to get comfortable. "It was okay, I guess. I spent a lot of time asleep."

"Yeah, I bet you were both tired." I moved away quickly, but she still managed to smack my arm. We both laughed. "I'm glad Father agreed to this," I told her as I listened to Cyrus and the children inside the small building to our left. They were all eager to speak to him, and he sounded excited to be there. "He's doing great."

Skye looked towards the building and uncrossed her arms. "You should have seen him with the kids from the orphanage."

"Did he tell you he met Will?"

Her head whipped toward me. "Oh yes, he did. He said hearing Will's beating heart was creepy. His words, not mine."

I nodded. "I get that. It was creepy to me, too—and confusing. As we walked back to the packhouse, I told him about Will and the time we'd spent together. Did he tell you what happened at the cliff?"

She shook her head. "We didn't talk about it much. My mother was around the entire time."

"You remember how Connor caught Will and me together, right? I asked Will about it, and he said he used an ability called compulsion to erase Connor's memory. He made Connor think I almost fell off the cliff."

Skye sat up. "Really? I didn't know vampires could do that."

"Only some of them can, apparently," I whispered. "I asked him about Keith as well, if he'd heard anything about it, but he said no. He also said vampires can't feed without biting their victims. So if the killer was a vampire, there would have been a mark left behind." I combed my fingers through my curls and pulled my hair into a bun before releasing it to fall over my shoulders. "Unfortunately, that means we're right back where we started. Because if it wasn't a vampire, then what was it?"

"This is getting scary. I wonder if whoever hurt Keith killed anyone else."

I glanced at Skye—I'd forgotten that I hadn't told her or Cyrus what my father said about the other murders. He had asked me not to say anything to anyone.

"There were other murders," I blurted, and her eyes widened as she turned to face me. "Do not tell a soul, do you understand me?" I looked around and we scooted closer together. "My father wants to keep it quiet, but . . . there were other supernaturals who died the same way Keith did. There have been similar murders in each town on the road to ours. That's why my father left. He's meeting with the other town leaders and an Enchanted the Werewolf Council sent. Whoever or whatever is killing these people is leaving no trace behind, not even a scent."

"Goddess," she drawled. "What the hell is going on?"

"Yeah," I said as I sighed, my eyes scanning the field of grass and flowers to our right. "Let's just hope that all of those leaders will put their heads together and come up with a way to solve this before it gets worse."

"I'm officially freaked out," Skye murmured by my side. "A supernatural going from town to town and killing, then leaving no trace behind? This is a real problem. We should tell Cyrus. I mean, he's always out and about. He can keep an eye out as well."

I nodded. "Sure, but he can't tell anyone, either. I mean, people need to know what's happening, but right now, there isn't much to tell. What we don't want is for people to panic. That would only make things worse."

The sound of footsteps grabbed our attention as Cyrus appeared outside with children—none more than eight years old—surrounding him. Their little voices all combined into a chorus of questions, but Cyrus was expertly answering them all in turn. When I glanced at Skye, I could see her pride and love for him shining in her eyes.

Cyrus finally looked our way and waved as we got to our feet. When another teacher appeared and told everyone it was time to go, he walked over to us.

"Hey," he said in greeting. "Sorry. I had to stay longer than expected."

"We heard," Skye said with a blush. "How was it?"

Cyrus's face lit up with one of his rare smiles. "It was great! I didn't expect the kids to be so interested, you know?"

"You made it fun for them," a she-wolf with a dazzling smile said from behind him. As she came to a stop in front of us, she placed her fist over her heart, then nodded at me and Skye in greeting.

We all offered her the same greeting. "Thank you, Haylen," Cyrus replied. My heart swelled at the pride in his voice. Haylen, her older sister Valentra, and their mother Ceila had dedicated their lives to educating the pups in our pack, and I was happy they were so open to having Cyrus work alongside them. "I'll be more prepared for a lesson tomorrow, so I'll . . ."

I looked his way just in time to see his eyes turn black.

"Cyrus, what's wrong?" Skye asked, placing her hand on his arm.

He covered her hand with his as he looked behind us, his gaze scanning the forest beyond the field. That's when I smelled it—a strong odor of sulfur in the air.

"What is that?" I asked, wiggling my nose. "Don't you smell that?" I asked Skye and Haylen, but they shook their heads.

"No, wait," Skye said, pulling her hand away to flick her finger under her nose. "What is that?"

"A supernatural maybe? Or an animal? It's like nothing I've ever smelled before." I stepped forward, my eyes narrowing on the tree line, but Cyrus pulled me back.

The sound of more children leaving for home drew our attention, but by then the smell in the air was strong enough that even they could smell it. A little girl with long curly brown hair screamed, and we all spun around to see a creature lumbering out of the forest.

"No," Cyrus said under his breath. He turned to Haylen as he began removing his shirt. "Get the kids home, now!" She didn't hesitate as she ran towards the four children frozen in fear. Then, he turned to Skye. "Send a warning to the others," he told her. She shifted immediately, ripping her dress to shreds, and within seconds, her piercing howl cut through the silence.

"That's a demon," Cyrus said, his voice deeper and more guttural as black smoke appeared around his body. "Well, not exactly a demon—an adracsas. But it's native to the Demon Realm."

"Then how the hell did it get here?" I asked, as Skye growled deeply.

The creature came to a stop in front of us, and I stared at its eyeless face with repulsion. Its skin was pale with black symbols covering various places on its body, and its shoulders were hunched. Black claws, maybe six inches long, protruded from its fingers.

My mouth turned downward, just now noticing something that looked like breasts hanging down its chest to its fat belly. But it was the cavernous mouth, devoid of any teeth or tongue, that made me uneasy.

Its mouth opened wide, and I covered my ears as it let out a deafening shriek. Cyrus stepped forward, his wings on full display, and he released a roar of his own in response. The power behind it stunned me for a moment, and the adracsas paused briefly as well.

"That's what killed Keith," Cyrus murmured.

For a moment, the world around me froze. I looked at the hairless creature. "Excuse me? How do you know?"

"The adracsas feeds by covering the face of a victim with its mouth and sucking the victim's blood out through their own mouth and nose. It's an agonizing death. In the Underworld, they send these creatures out as bounty hunters."

"Bounty hunters?" I repeated.

"Yes, which means someone sent it here for a reason. And I have a good idea why. Watch out for the claws!"

The previously slow-moving demon burst into action with unexpected speed, charging towards us as its shrieks filled the air. Cyrus took to the sky as Skye rushed forward to meet the creature head-on. I began shifting, allowing the pain of my bones breaking to roll through me.

Now on all fours, I howled long and hard, telling any wolf in the vicinity to stay back. I doubted any Werewolf Guards close by would heed the warning, but I didn't think there were many of them around. With the storm over, most of the pack had ventured into the town, picking up enough food for a few days in case the storm wasn't finished with us yet.

I lunged forward, my paws hitting the ground hard as Skye was slapped to the side by the creature's large hand. From the sky, Cyrus dove onto the creature but had to retreat as its black claws swiped at him, too.

The adracsas was defending itself well—too well. I growled at Skye, and she growled back as she got to her feet. We began circling the demon, our growls blending with the strange clicking sounds it was making. Of course, not having eyes, it probably used either smell or sound—or both—to track its prey.

I heard Cyrus's wings flapping loudly above us. As I looked up at him, I noted his tightly clenched fists. I knew after we took care of this, he'd be leaving us. Lives were lost because of this thing, and he'd stop at nothing to find out who had sent it.

The creature held its head back as if listening to Cyrus's wings, then unexpectedly charged at Skye. As she moved right, it grabbed her by the face and threw her with astonishing strength. She flew through the air and landed with a thud, knocking her unconscious.

I ran forward, looking for an opening, but the adracsas was suddenly engulfed by black smoke. I skidded to a halt and looked up to the sky. Black smoke was seeping out of

Cyrus, and the markings on his body were moving up onto his face.

The demon's cry made my ears feel as if they were bleeding, and I looked down to see it levitating off the ground, its enormous hands swiping at the smoke.

"Check on her," Cyrus said, his voice a rumble of a thousand voices. "Give me space."

I rushed to Skye, who had shifted back into her human form—though she remained unconscious. She didn't budge when I nudged her face with my snout. I stood over her body as the creature's cries grew louder. The black cloud surrounding it finally dissipated, and it fell to the ground, its arms flailing wildly. Cyrus shot downward from the sky like a bullet, and a horrific screech exploded from the demon's mouth when Cyrus's hand pierced its chest as they both slammed to the ground.

He killed it so easily.

Cyrus stood up, his wings flapping once more before disappearing into his back. Black blood now drenched his hand. His chest was rising and falling rapidly as he studied the dead thing beneath him. He bared his fangs as he growled, half of his face still covered in symbols similar to the ones on the creature he had just killed.

The darkness I'd felt when he had rushed home with Skye not so long ago sizzled through the air. He shook his hand to remove some of the very pungent blood and walked over to me. His red eyes returned to gray again as he stared at Skye. I stepped back from covering her with my body.

"Someone sent it here for me." He looked down at his hand and the muscles near his jaw tightened.

"It killed people from other towns, not just Keith," I told

him, shifting back into my human form. "So what are you saying?"

"It was tracking my scent. Didn't you notice that its focus was mostly on me? It charged at me, it kept turning its head upwards towards me . . . The acute sense of smell and sharp hearing allow the adracsas to track its prey easily, but it's slow." He shook his head. "If it killed others, chances are they came into contact with me, just like Keith did the night he died." His lips pulled back from his fangs as he growled and turned away for a moment. "It doesn't have eyes, so it kills anything with the scent it's tracking. When its prey is dead, the scent should fade. If it doesn't, the adracsas keeps tracking."

"You're leaving, aren't you?" I asked, and he looked at me over his shoulder. Slits appeared vertically on either side of his back, and his wings pierced through.

"Yes. I don't know when I'll be back, but someone has to pay for this. Burn the body."

I watched as he pushed off the ground. The surrounding snow blew into my face, but I didn't look away until I could no longer see him, his red wings vanishing in the clouds.

Skye groaned, finally waking up. As she sluggishly reached up to hold the side of her head, I sat down beside her. I sighed, staring at the dead demon a few feet away from us.

"This isn't over, Skye." I closed my eyes and listened to the sound of wolves rushing towards us. "I have a feeling things are about to get really, really interesting."

8

CYRUS

I stormed through my mother's castle, ignoring the demons scurrying to get out of my way. In my human form, my eyes were as red as flames—a gift from my father. Obviously, everyone knew I was pissed.

The day those humans hurt Skye, something within me was set free. A power or maybe just a darkness I hadn't even known was there was released—including red eyes, just like my father's. Ever since then, I'd noticed a burst in my strength . . . and in my hunger.

I'd been keeping that hunger under control with Skye's help, but feeding on her caused me more pain. I wanted her —I wanted every inch of her—but she wasn't ready. I'd wait forever for her if I could, but I didn't have that kind of time. I had yet to tell her about the three years I had left with her, and my wish for her to join me in the Demon Realm.

Maybe it was cowardice, but the possibility that she might say no terrified me. With everything going on with Elinor getting married and leaving sooner rather than later, telling Skye I'd be doing the same would surely break her heart.

I threw my mother's office doors open and found the room empty.

Someone down here sent that adracsas after me—I knew it. I turned around and spotted one of her human pets. The girl's green eyes widened with fear.

"Where is my mother?" I asked. When she started trembling, I added, "I won't hurt you. Just tell me where she is."

"T-the garden, she's in the garden."

I walked away, the sound of the girl's pounding heart echoing in my ears. Whoever had sent the demon must have known it would be no match for me. So why did they send it? If the goal wasn't to have it kill me, but instead to have it kill others because of me, it certainly succeeded.

My mother's garden was beautiful, with flowers of all colors—all of them deadly, of course. I released my power as I entered, causing the flowers to wither as I walked by them. My mother, as well as a few of my siblings and other demons who were all lounging by a large fountain, turned to me.

My mother's facial expression remained calm and neutral, but her eyes burned with rage as she watched her beautiful flowers die. "Cyrus, what's the meaning of this?" she asked calmly.

"Who sent it?" My lips barely moved, but my voice echoed throughout the garden. My eyes fell on my oldest brother, Baxton, and three of my other siblings who were born after I'd left the Demon Realm—triplet girls that I'd never spoken to. There were about twenty demons hanging around, some with hatred in their eyes, some with fear, but I didn't care. What I needed right now were answers.

"I won't ask again," I growled, watching in satisfaction as the remaining flowers in the garden wilted.

My mother sighed as she stood up, pushing her black hair braided with roses over her shoulder. "Darling, what are you talking about?"

"Someone sent a bounty hunter to Earth," I answered, my eyes moving from her to the others. "A boy I knew lost his life, among many others. Was it you?"

Her perfectly shaped brow arched. "Excuse me? Do I look like I have time for such idleness? I'm going to need you to calm down, Cyrus. You're killing my blooms. What does one boy's death have to do with anyone here?"

My teeth clenched as a raging storm began at my core. Thunder echoed above her garden and black clouds drew close. I was powerful on Earth, but here, where there was more magic in the air, my strength was almost unmatched.

"I'm not on Earth," I answered calmly. "I don't need to hold back here." My mother's face fell, obviously realizing I was serious. "I want to know who sent the demon. Either you tell me, or I'm going to tear everyone limb from limb until I find who did it." Lightning struck the ground, causing some of the demons to gasp in fear.

"Wow, look at you, showcasing your little gifts," Baxton said, smirking as he stood up. His honey-gold eyes moved up and down my body as he crossed his arms over his chest.

I should have known he was the one who sent the hunter. Baxton considered me his rival ever since we were little, and it looked as if his hatred towards me had finally gotten out of hand. He'd always despised me more than any of my other siblings because even though he was the firstborn, our mother declared that I'd be inheriting her Legion. Not him.

It was no surprise Baxton and Orias were close. They had a lot in common.

"Looks like you're not as weak as I thought you were," he said, uncrossing his arms. "Defeating a bounty hunter is no big deal, though." When I clenched my fists, he quickly added, "Relax, brother. It was merely a joke. I wanted to see how the great Cyrus would react to a little chaos in his perfect world. So, were any of your werewolf whores hurt?"

If I hadn't been there, everyone in the pack who carried my scent would have died. And the demon would have gone for the person with the strongest scent first—Skye. Thankfully, the bounty hunter only knocked her unconscious. And even that was too much for me to handle.

But I would take care of it. The thunder above us stopped as I forced the angry crease between my brows to vanish. I inhaled deeply, and the smile on Baxton's face faded. He did all of this to provoke me, to see me lash out.

I wouldn't give him the satisfaction of seeing me angry, but if he wanted a fight, I was more than ready for him. Years of practice had taught me how to hold my rage within me—but that only made it more powerful.

Baxton's jaw clenched as his gold eyes turned black. I might not appear angry anymore, but my brother was no fool. He knew what I felt right now was much worse than what I was letting on.

Our mother backed away, her red-painted lips curving at the corner. This was nothing more than entertainment for her.

Baxton ran towards me, a golden dagger materializing in his hand—only I vanished before his eyes. Baxton stopped, then spun around when I reappeared behind him. My hand shot out, grabbing his face, but he stabbed me in the gut.

I barely felt the pain as I squeezed his face and threw him to the ground, cracking the earth with the impact. He stared at me wide-eyed as I pulled the dagger from my gut and threw it to the ground. My mother gasped as my blood, red and bubbling like lava, spilled out and burned the earth.

"So much like our King," she muttered.

Baxton gritted his teeth as his fangs and claws appeared. The second his body twitched—a sign that he was going to attack me again—my wings burst from my back as lightning struck him.

Grabbing his face, I watched and listened as my brother wailed in pain. Skye, Elinor . . . the entire pack could have died because my brother couldn't let go of his grudge. I glanced at my mother. The sight of her wide eyes filled with admiration made my stomach turn. I narrowed my eyes as her lips stretched into a smile. No, I was wrong. It wasn't admiration I saw in her eyes—it was obsession.

"Did your father tell you how long you have left?" my mother asked, her eyes alight with excitement.

The other demons around us, the ones who had been watching my clash with Baxton, now looked on with a combination of fear and fascination. "Yes, I'll be returning in three years," I said. Her face dropped—I guessed she didn't think it would be that long. "Orders from the King himself," I added as my eyes changed back to gray. I looked Baxton's way, now that his crying had stopped. His hand fell away from his face, revealing a wound down his left eye. "I'll be taking over the Legion then," I said. Then, leaning forward, I added, "And you'll be my *faithful* subject. The next time you think it would be a good idea to piss me off, Baxton, please remember that."

"Baxton was onto something if all it takes to anger you is to send a demon your way," my mother chuckled to herself.

We stared at each other for a moment, the air between us sizzling with tension. Then I stepped over my brother to stand before her. "If you're thinking of doing the same, Mother, I'd advise against it." Her perfectly smooth face wrinkled as her brows pulled together.

"You might be a Sin and the current leader of this Legion, but I surpassed you in power long ago. Do you want to know how?" I leaned forward and placed my lips against her ear. "Because you never cared about me or anyone else. All you worried about was yourself." I pulled away. "I might not have trained here in the Demon Realm, but don't worry about my skills. I learned control over my hunger without your help, didn't I?" Her eyes widened at that, and I kissed her cheek before turning away.

"You cocky little shit," she hissed, and I stopped, keeping my back to her. "Do you think I have to give you my Legion? I have many children, Cyrus, many. There's nothing that says you have to be the next in line."

"I think that decision was taken out of your hands the moment you made me attend that ball," I said, inhaling deeply. Of course, that was a disadvantage for me as well. Because now that I had my father's eyes on me, I had to take over the Legion if he demanded it. I might be stronger than my mother, but I was nowhere near strong enough to defy him . . . yet. "I'll be spending my last three years on Earth in peace. And when I come back, I'd rather you give up control of the Legion peacefully. I'd hate to have to kill you to get it."

I could feel her power flare as I kept walking. But I ignored it, along with the shocked whispers from the other demons. No one knew the suffering I went through, the things I was forced to do when I left the pack to learn to control my power and hunger. To spare Elinor and Skye the details of the awful things I did, I'd locked that part of my past away.

But if my mother hurt the people I loved on Earth and I became the heartless demon she always wanted because of it, she'd live to regret it.

Skye

After I'd finished cleaning my room and helping Mother with dinner, I ventured outside to sit on the back porch Cyrus built for me. I'd told him once how I'd love to have a place I could relax and just stare at the stars, and he started building the porch for me a week later. It took him two weeks to finish it all on his own, but he told me it was worth it. We'd spent countless nights here since, chatting as we admired the night sky.

And I found another use for it, one I considered even more critical. Because each time he visited the Demon Realm, I sat on the little bench he made and waited for him to come back. Since time moved a little faster in the Underworld, a day here could be a week there. Whenever days or weeks passed here without his return, it often left me wondering if he was coming back at all.

Still, we both knew that I'd wait here forever just to see him return safely.

Although I loved him, I didn't deceive myself. I knew he was a demon from the Demon Realm, but Earth had always been his true home. It took us so long, so many years to admit our feelings for each other. Thinking back now, I shook my head at my own foolishness. How could I not have seen that he shared my feelings? Groaning, I held my head. I knew he had to leave. He had no other option. His mother would stop at nothing to make sure he took over her Legion.

So, what's going to happen to us?

That was the question that had plagued me for years. But I already had the answer, already knew how the story ended between us—and I hated it. He and I would never be able to make a relationship between us public. I'd only hold him back if he stayed here, trapping him in a secret relationship or trapping us both in an agonizing existence of being just friends.

This was just too complicated.

I had no idea what our relationship actually was. We'd admitted our feelings to each other, I allowed him to feed on me, we flirted and kissed . . . But what were we?

"What are you thinking so hard about?" I jumped to my feet, my heart skipping a beat as I stared into Cyrus's bright eyes, glowing like candle flames in the darkness. The side of his mouth curved as he stepped onto the porch and walked over to me. "Did you miss me?"

I hugged him, and he responded immediately, crushing me to his body. "I'll take that as a yes."

"How long were you down there? It's been three days

here," I said as we remained in each other's arms, his heart-beat thumping in my ear.

"Four days." He pulled back and pushed a strand of my hair behind my ear. "Are you okay?"

"I'm fine," I answered softly. "Did you find who sent the demon?"

He guided me over to the bench, and we both sat down. "I did. It was my eldest brother."

"Why?"

"Why else? To provoke me, of course." He crossed his legs. "He won't be doing anything like that again, though."

"What did you do?" I asked, not sure if I really wanted to know. But he merely glanced at me and smiled. I rolled my eyes. "Fine, keep your secrets."

I crossed my arms and tilted my head upward to stare at the night sky. But I could see him watching me in my peripheral vision.

He laughed. "We fought," he finally said, and I turned back to him. The smile on his lips slowly faded and his brows pulled together for a moment. "And I won. Then I spoke to my mother for a moment before heading back. I, um . . ." He stood up and walked away. "There's something I've been meaning to talk to you about, I just haven't . . ."

I felt my chest tightened with panic. Somehow, I knew I wouldn't like what he was about to say.

He turned back to face me. "I have three years left on Earth."

I said nothing—I couldn't have even if I'd wanted to. We stared at each other for a moment before I finally looked away, his words swimming around in my mind.

"Three years?" I asked, and he hummed his response. "Your mother, right?"

"Yes. When I went to my father's ball, he made it a point to find me." I looked at him. That was one detail he had most definitely left off when he had told me about his visit.

"He was the one who told me I had to return in three years. And he wasn't just telling me, Skye. It was a command. And unlike my mother's, this is one I can't disobey." He sat back down beside me. "I've wanted to tell you since I returned, but—"

"I get it," I interjected. "I understand why you didn't."

"Because of the look on your face right now, yes."

I gave him a tight-lipped smile, and he chuckled. "I, um, I don't think I'll be able to come back once I leave."

"Yeah, I get that, too." I bit down on my lip as I tried to get a handle on my emotions.

I had been thinking about this before he returned. I always knew that one day he'd have to leave, but that didn't stop me from bursting into tears. He gathered me in his arms, holding me as I sobbed.

Elinor was pretty much set to leave with Elijah, and now Cyrus would be leaving as well. With the Alpha gone and the announcement of Elinor's marriage on hold, I'd tried not to speak of the matter too much with her. Especially once I knew she'd been seeing that vampire, Will. I couldn't imagine how angry I'd be if my mother told me she was marrying me off to someone she chose for me—especially if that someone wasn't my mate.

It still shocked me that the Alpha was doing such a thing —forcing his daughter to marry someone who wasn't her mate. Maybe Elinor had been right to think that he was just trying to get her married off. Why else would he arrange a marriage for her?

The entire thing was hypocritical to me. Werewolves frowned upon non-mated relationships, and there was a good reason for it. And yet, the Alpha had broken that rule. But if anyone ever discovered Elinor's friendship with Will, all hell would break loose.

I sighed.

Elinor was stubborn. I knew that better than anyone, so I was sure she'd be able to handle whatever the Alpha threw at her. And I had to deal with Cyrus leaving in the same way. We were all adults, and I could fully accept the way things had to be. Even so, it had always been the three of us through thick and thin. Now, one of us would move to another pack, and the other—the only man I'd ever loved—would disappear from my life forever.

My eyes widened at that thought, and I pulled away from him. I'd never admitted to myself that I loved him—but of course, I did. How could I not? I turned to look at him. His eyes were filled with so much regret and pain. And it reminded me that this decision had to be eating away at him as well.

I dried my tears quickly. "I, um . . . sorry. I knew you'd have to leave eventually, but hey, three years isn't right now. We have time." I frowned as he looked away. "We have time, right?"

"I'm leaving the pack as soon as possible." He reached out and held my hand. "I handled my brother, but I angered my mother in the process. If I stayed here, I'd be putting you and the entire pack in danger."

"So you're leaving now? You can't do that, Cyrus." I

suddenly felt panicked. "Werewolves aren't weaklings! We can protect ourselves from anything your mother or brother or anyone else throws at us."

"People died because of me, Skye. A young member of your pack died merely because he spoke to me. And I can't guarantee I'll always be here to help if something happens. There are things in the Demon Realm that not even the Alpha could handle. I'm a prince of Hell, Skye. I don't belong here to begin with."

I sobered up at that, and the anger I was feeling faded. He was speaking the truth, I knew, but it was hard to accept. I sighed, defeated. "Where will you go?"

He ran his thumb across the back of my hand. "I have wings, remember? I can go anywhere I wish."

I pulled my hand away. "Yes, but where will you stay? You need a home." I got up and walked away. "You'll need a roof over your head, Cyrus. You can't fly around for three years. Y-you have to feed." My eyes widened as a burst of jealousy made my head spin with wild thoughts. I turned to face him. "How will you feed?"

He walked over . . . and kissed me. His hands shot out and cupped my cheeks before I could even react. Instantly my mind cleared of the tortured thoughts I was having, and I sagged against him, reveling in the feeling of having his arms wrapped around me.

Safe. That was how I felt when he held me, and I squeezed my eyes against the thought of him leaving. Finally, I broke our kiss and rested my head against his chest. We stood there in each other's arms, not wanting the moment to end.

"I love you," he whispered, burying his face in my hair. My body froze, my heart hammering away inside my chest, and a smile slowly blossomed on my lips as I pulled him closer. "I always have, but I've been a coward. I feared that I'd ruin our friendship if I told you and you didn't feel the same," he added.

I pulled back, my lips parting to say something, but he placed a finger against them. "Listen. I'll be coming back from time to time to see you—and Elinor as well. You two mean everything to me. But I need to use the three years I have left here before I have to leave permanently, so I thought I'd travel to a few places I've been wanting to see. Maybe I'll accept Theanos's invitation to visit his father's kingdom. I've never even seen a dragon."

"Yeah, neither have I," I grumbled. "You're going to be miserable without me," I told him, and he laughed.

"You're right about that." Pinching my chin, he tilted my head back. "But I'm sure I can work something out so you can visit. Um, would you?"

I nodded right away. "Of course! Are you kidding?" I tilted my head to the side, narrowing my eyes when he suddenly got tense. "Cyrus?"

"Would you come with me, then? Would you live there with me?"

I stepped out of his arms, not exactly clear what he was asking.

He looked down at me, as if he was trying to gauge my reaction. "It's not as bad as I always portray it. There are beautiful places in the Underworld—places I wish I could have run away to as a child. But I came here instead, and I don't regret that. My point is, it's not all dark clouds and crazed demons."

I wasn't expecting that. "Cyrus, I can't decide that now." I pointed towards the house. "I mean, my mother is here, and . . . I can't make that decision now."

I saw the disappointment in his eyes before it vanished under an unreadable expression. "No, I understand. I shouldn't have just sprung that on you."

Shaking my head, I walked over and took his hands in mine. "I said I can't decide right now, but I didn't say no." I couldn't hide the laugh that slipped from my lips as his face lit up.

"Do you feel the same about me?"

I closed my eyes for a moment. There was a time when the thought of confessing my attraction to Cyrus scared the hell out of me. He'd told me he loved me so easily, like the future didn't scare him at all. Then why should I be afraid?

"I do," I answered. As I opened my eyes, I gazed up at him —the man who'd been the most important person in my life from the moment we met, from the moment he'd saved my life the first time. He'd proven his feelings for me with more than just words. "I do love you, Cyrus. I always have. And nothing will ever change that. But I am going to need you to tell me how you plan on feeding."

He broke out laughing as I arched a brow, waiting for his response. He suddenly leaned forward and kissed my neck, sending a chill down my spine. Then he pulled my earlobe between his teeth as he snaked his hands around my waist.

"I'll return whenever I need to feed. So, knowing that—" He kissed the spot just beneath my ear, and my eyes fluttered closed again. "Be prepared."

9

ELINOR

"Are you going to tell me where we're going?"

Will stopped walking and turned to me. He reached out and pinched my chin, tilting my head back gently.

"It's a surprise," he answered before leaning in to kiss me. But I pulled away.

His hand fell away from my chin as he smirked, then turned and continued walking. Goddess, I wanted to kiss him, but things had been moving way too fast between us. I had promised to marry Elijah, yet here I was, following a gorgeous vampire who I very much wanted to kiss through a forest on my way to Goddess-knew-where.

What the hell am I going to do about this?

As soon as my father returned, so would Elijah, and my engagement would then become official. My father sent word two days ago that he'd be back in a few days and that the Enchanted with him had a vision that the pack was under attack. My mother sent a letter back to him, telling him about everything that had happened and giving him the good news that Keith's killer had been dealt with.

Since he hadn't replied, he must be on his way home. We'd solved the problem—the whole purpose of attending the meeting to begin with—right here in our pack. A part of me wished it hadn't all happened the way it had because Cyrus's announcement that he'd be leaving the pack broke my heart.

As hard as it was for me, I recognized that it was much worse for Skye. It had taken me an hour to convince Cyrus to stay for a few extra days so we could have a proper farewell party for him—just the three of us. And I really wanted him to stay until my father returned so he could say goodbye to Cyrus as well. A part of me was honestly hoping my father would do a better job of convincing him not to leave at all.

"Hey." Will held onto my arm. "You seem distant."

We stopped walking, and I looked up at the night sky. "There is just so much going on right now." I looked at him, admiring his unusual blue eyes for a moment. "I don't think I'll ever get used to your eyes being blue and not red like most vampires."

"You'll get used to it," he replied with a shrug.

I gave him a tight-lipped smile. "I shouldn't be doing this."

"Taking a stroll with a friend?"

"Taking a secret stroll with a vampire, smartass. And hanging around a she-wolf is a bad idea for you, too. Won't your kind lose it, if they find out?"

"I know I'm a smartass, thank you very much," he replied with a smirk.

"I'm being serious," I told him, poking him in the chest.

His expression became solemn as he removed two small vials from his pocket. "I know you're serious, Elinor. And yes, the other vampires would be furious." He looked around us, his eyes scanning the forest. "They despise werewolves. Your Guards have killed many of our kind. But let's not think about that now. We've come far enough. For tonight, Little Wolf, I don't want you to think about what's happening now or what might happen in the future. Okay?"

I made a face. "Yeah, right. My brain is allergic to relaxing. I have to think about everything past, present, and future at all times. I have no choice."

He softly chuckled as he brought out two vials of liquid from his pocket and held up the red one for me to see. I stared at the swirling solution, entranced. "Do you trust me, Elinor?"

When I gave him a blank look, he shook his head, pulling the stopper and tossing the vial on the ground a few feet away from us. I backed away quickly as a whirling crimson portal appeared. He held his hand out to me. "Trust me."

He wants me to leave the forest with him!

"Will, I—" I protested.

But he stepped towards the portal, his hand still outstretched to me. "Please, trust me."

I swallowed hard as I looked around us. He was smart to take us so far into the forest. Any supernatural within a mile of us would've easily detected the energy coming from the portal.

"I assume the other vial I saw will bring us back here?" I asked, and he nodded.

I slid my hand into his before I could change my mind. What was I doing? Could I trust him? Then again, after all this time, why would he hurt me now? He'd had plenty of chances in the past.

Still, my heart hammered in my chest as he led me towards the portal. He squeezed my hand reassuringly, no doubt sensing my anxiety.

Half of his body entered the portal, then he looked back at me and pulled me closer. I didn't protest as he snaked his hand around my waist and pinned me to his side as we entered the portal together.

I closed my eyes as a bright light engulfed us. I noticed immediately that I felt the same way I did when Cyrus carried me on his back. It felt like Will and I were floating through the air, and my skin dotted with goosebumps at the amount of raw energy around us.

However, it lasted for only a few seconds. Then Will tightened his hold around my waist, and we stepped out of the portal together.

I opened my eyes and was stunned by what I saw before me. I looked at Will and saw he was grinning. The portal at our backs vanished, and I walked forward into this new place, my eyes moving around rapidly as I took in my surroundings.

Night had turned into day, and the dark beauty of the forest we'd left behind was nothing compared to the one I was now standing in.

"Th-this is . . . incredible," I said under my breath, holding my hand out to the most beautiful butterfly I'd ever seen.

The butterfly's wings were a bright blend of red and

orange with two long, feather-like tails at its back like a hummingbird. It landed on my finger, its wings fluttering slowly. I watched as it turned a light blue and green before flitting away again.

Everywhere I looked, the world seemed awash in brilliant colors and light. Above us, the light blue, pale pink, and orange hues of the sky reminded me of a giant watercolor painting. Even the forest was incandescent—the trees, animals, and insects all glowed. An animal cried in the distance and was immediately answered by another. I turned to Will and found him watching me.

"What is this place?"

He walked over to me and handed me a flower. I took it timidly because its red petals were moving in and out rhythmically, as if it were breathing. I froze as the petals slowly morphed into wings, and before I knew it, I was staring down at a small, green-eyed lizard.

"I've never seen a lizard with wings," I said. The lizard jumped out of my hand, startling me, and I watched in wonder as its wings swiftly carried it away. "Will, where are we?"

"Dragon Territory," he answered.

My face fell. "Have you completely lost your mind?" I reached into his pocket for the second vial, and he grabbed my wrist. "Let go of me. If you're into getting burnt to a crisp, then good for you. But that's not what I signed up for!" He pulled my hand out of his pocket and laughed. I just stood there, staring at him, not sure just what I'd gotten myself into. "You're a madman."

"Elinor, calm down." He continued laughing as he walked around me. "I know dragons are even more territorial than wolves are, but the dragon who governs *this* land is a friend of mine." He inhaled deeply, his eyes closing for a moment, and when they reopened, they flashed red for a moment before returning to blue. "We'll be fine. So relax. You look a little panicked."

"A little?!" I said.

In response, he walked over to me, took my hand, and began pulling me through the forest.

It was hard to stay tense as I took in everything around us. The forest was alive with so much life and light that it made it hard to focus on just one thing. I pulled on Will's hand when I spotted a tiny black and white cat with two tails sleeping on a rock. Her white tail swished steadily while her black one remained still. Sensing our presence, she opened her eyes, revealing one green iris and one blue one. She mewed loudly, then jumped off the rock and strolled over to us.

I chuckled as I stooped down to pet her. "What are you complaining about?" I asked as the cat rubbed herself against my hand, then walked away to do the same to Will.

I blinked rapidly. The rest of the cat's pure white fur darkened to black as she returned to her napping spot on the rock.

"I come here when I need to relax, but the chance to get away rarely presents itself," Will said.

"How are you friends with a dragon? It would have to be a noble if they govern this land, right?" I thought for a moment. "Do you know Theanos? He's half-dragon, isn't he?"

"He is," he answered. "But his father is the King of the dragons. My friend is just a noble, as you said, but that—"

His words were cut short as a dragon flew above the

forest. It was massive, and my mouth fell open at the size of the shadow it cast over the forest. I kept my eyes on the blue-scaled creature until I could no longer see it, but the wind created from its wings was blowing everything violently. I staggered, trying to keep my footing.

"Goddess," I murmured when the wind died down. "Do you think it saw us?"

"She," Will said, walking away as if nothing had happened. "And I'm sure she did."

"How do you know it was a female?" I asked, hurrying to catch up to him.

"Her size. Female dragons are much smaller than males."

Nodding in acknowledgment, I couldn't help but wonder how Theanos's mother had managed to get pregnant. I shook my head and forced the images that were popping up in my head back into the dark recesses of my mind with a shudder.

"Hey, um, I meant to tell you, I'm sorry about what happened with Cyrus. And also, I apologize if it seemed as if I was accusing you of having something to do with Keith's death."

He waved his hand dismissively before pushing his hair back from his face. I watched as the long strands fell down his back, and my stomach clenched at the thought of running my fingers through it the way he had.

"Don't worry about it. I heard you found the creature responsible?"

"More like it found us," I grumbled. "But yeah. Cyrus took care of it."

"Good," he said, nodding. "Now follow me. I want to show you something."

"You're showing me a lot already," I joked. "But okay."

We walked in silence while I admired the forest and its strange creatures until a large white tree came into view. It was as large as an oak tree but wider, and its branches had what looked like white hair hanging from it. As we drew closer, I realized it was just the tree's leaves hanging down on vines.

"The Dragons call this tree a weeping willow. Dragons considered it a symbol of peace," Will explained as I bent under one of the long vines to avoid being hit in the face. Once we were underneath the tree, it was as if the weather had changed from being semi-warm to cool. But I could feel the aura of peace throughout the forest coming from the tree as well.

"Oh," I drawled, looking up. "It's beautiful."

"Look at this." He reached out and placed his hand against the tree's trunk. Within seconds, the tree glowed bright red where his hand had touched it.

"Wow," I gushed, moving closer. "What was that?"

"It reacts to the aura of anyone who touches it," he explained, then pulled his hand away. "Try it. It won't bite. Actually, very few things here do."

"Then I guess we know why you don't live here," I said with a snicker.

The side of his mouth curved in a devilish smirk. "You're right. But I can bite gently if you ask me to." He took a step towards me, his eyes narrowing as they turned red. My stomach clenched as his gaze wandered to my lips, then to my neck, and finally to my chest. "I can show you if you'd like."

I reached out to grab hold of the tree, needing to steady myself against his sudden charm. When I touched the bark, the tree started to glow a pale blue. I smiled excitedly. My aura appeared so peaceful and serene, and I silently thanked the tree for the distraction.

However, I frowned, and so did Will, when the light faded —even though I hadn't pulled my hand away. I opened my mouth to ask him why when the entire tree started to radiate white light. I tried to pull away, but my hand felt glued to the trunk. When the leaves began to shake, I panicked.

"Will, is this supposed to happen?" I yelled as the light pulsated and the shaking grew worse. "Will?"

He placed both of his hands on the tree. It flared red around his hands, and whatever held me to the tree finally released me. I scrambled away, putting some distance between myself and the tree.

"What was that?" Will mumbled.

My fear turned to anger. "Are you kidding? I should be asking you that. You're the expert here!"

"He doesn't have an answer for you. Even I have never seen the tree light up like that." I stepped back as a woman appeared out of nowhere. She stood with her hands behind her back as she focused on me.

Her green eyes had vertical pupils like a cat's. But despite her strange eyes, she was breathtaking. She was tall —taller even than my 5'7"—and was wearing a simple blue gown with a long train. She looked towards the tree, a smile growing on her pink lips before her eyes returned to me.

"What's a beautiful woman like you doing with the likes of Will?" she asked, walking over to me.

I glanced at Will, who stood there with an amused look on his face. He wasn't usually so expressive, but I'd noticed how much more relaxed he became after we stepped out from the portal.

"I'm not so bad, and she knows that," he told the woman, and she rolled her eyes.

But she caught me off guard by grabbing my hand. And I tensed as she closed her eyes.

"Elu, you're freaking her out," Will said to the woman.

She opened her eyes again. "Hmm, interesting," she murmured with a grin. But it disappeared as her expression grew serious. She glared at Will. "You haven't returned in over a year."

Then she looked my way and smiled again. "It's nice to meet you, Elinor. I'm Elu, daughter of Aregon, the noble who owns these lands. I've never met a werewolf before."

She's a dragon! Oh, of course. Apparently, they could shift into human-like forms. Werewolves really knew very little about dragons in general since we rarely came in contact with any.

"It's nice to meet you, Elu. But how do you know my name?"

She moved her strawberry blond curls over her shoulder. "Your touch told me a lot about you. Are you ready?" she asked Will. He nodded.

This girl is all over the place.

"Good, everything is prepared," she told us as she turned and began walking away. I looked Will's way for an explanation, but he merely took my hand, urging me to follow her.

We walked in silence as Elu led us somewhere. I still didn't know where we were going, but I found that I didn't really care. I glanced at Will, realizing that I had managed not to think about all my problems waiting for me back home for the past hour. Until now, I hadn't worried about my father, or getting married, or Cyrus leaving.

I'd always wanted to leave my pack and explore Earth. Thanks to Will, I was finally getting the chance. I'd never felt this free before. Here, it didn't matter at all that I was the firstborn daughter of an Alpha. Right now, I was just a girl exploring a forest in Dragon Territory with my special friend.

"Here," Elu announced, and my breath caught as she pointed to a large pond with a towering tree at its center. Beneath the tree was a table and two chairs. As Elu waved her hand, the pond rocks floated to the surface to create a path to the tree.

"What is this?" I asked Will, who was watching me closely.

"Our first date, Little Wolf. I think it's about time we sat down together instead of sneaking around in a forest."

"Well, we're still in a forest," I told him, and Elu giggled. "But I like this one more."

"That's good to hear. Dragons are spiritual creatures. Because of that, our lands flourish with life and beauty." Elu held her hand out towards the pond once more, and I noted the dazzling gold bracelet on her wrist. Next to her casual attire, the bracelet really stood out. I could tell that it was pure gold and must have cost a fortune. "Please, both of you enjoy yourself," she urged. "The plates have been spelled so whatever meal you wish to have will appear in front of you."

"Thank you." I placed my fist over my heart as I bowed, and she smiled widely before nodding to us both.

"You're welcome, Elinor. I hope to see you again someday without Will so we girls can chat."

"I don't get why you insist on pretending you hate me," Will grumbled by my side, though his blue eyes twinkled.

Elu winked at him and then turned away.

"Shall we?" Will asked as he held his hand out to me. I slid my hand into his.

He led me across the pond. When we reached the table, he pulled out my chair for me before sitting down himself. As Elu had said, the moment I thought of a meal, it appeared on my plate. I watched as the gold goblet beside my plate filled itself with wine.

Will held his goblet out to me, and I tapped mine against his. "Thank you for this," I told him. He just picked up my hand and kissed the back of it.

We didn't speak as we ate in comfortable silence. I was too transfixed by the food and the music of the forest to talk anyway. After we finished eating, our plates vanished and our goblets refilled themselves.

"Can I just move here?" I joked as I sipped my wine. "Self-filling goblets are definitely a win in my book."

"The Dragon Territories are rich with magic, allowing dragons to do amazing things. You can feel it, can't you?" He held his hand out as if touching something.

"I can," I answered. "I've felt it from the moment we arrived." I held my head back as I gazed up at the tree above us and the colorful birds perched on the branches. "I can see myself living here. It's beautiful."

"Yes," Will answered softly, and I looked his way to see his lowered eyes on me. "I agree."

We stared at each other for a moment until I cleared my throat and looked away. I didn't need to get lost in his eyes.

We'd never get another opportunity to talk like this without being interrupted. "You know I'm engaged, right?"

He nodded. "Yes, to an Alpha-born named Elijah."

"Then you know we . . ." I trailed off, trying to find the right words. "We can never do this again. Wait, how do you know his name? I never told you, did I?"

"You didn't," He gazed at me from over the rim of his goblet. "I have my ways."

I narrowed my eyes as he lowered his goblet and licked his lips. The wind blew gently around us. I reclined in my chair as we simply stared at each other. Will didn't look at all bothered that I was getting married. He'd brought me here knowing that. He either didn't have feelings for me the way I thought he did, or he didn't care that I was promised to someone else.

I looked down at my lap. Of course, he didn't care. "It doesn't bother you that I'm getting married to someone else?"

"Are you even sure you're getting married? From what I've heard, nothing has been officially announced. And Elijah isn't your mate." He exhaled, then placed his elbows on the table and leaned forward. "If you had found your mate, you wouldn't be here with me. So, no. I don't care that you're getting married to Elijah. And if you marry him, we'll still—" His eyes darted to my lips for a moment before returning to my eyes. "We'll still be able to be friends."

"You would be glad I haven't found my mate," I grumbled.

He dared to nod his head. "Of course, I am."

"Well, even so, we can't . . . you can't kiss me anymore. That's what I'm saying. It's not right," I said in a rush. The side of his mouth curved as he tilted his head. "I mean it,

Will." He nodded but didn't look at all as if he was listening to me.

Rolling my eyes, I looked away, frowning when I spotted something moving from behind a flower on the pond. This was so confusing. There was a part of me that was happy I hadn't met my mate yet either. And as much as he called this thing between us *friendship*, friends didn't kiss the way we did. If I had found my mate, I knew the butterflies I felt whenever I saw Will would disappear.

Still, I wouldn't be *that* woman—the one who snuck around with one man while she was married to another.

"I know what it feels like to have things forced on you, to have decisions made about your life that you don't want," he said. I looked over at Will reclined in his chair, his eyes reflecting the slightest bit of anger. I saw it—I saw a similar frustration with his own life. "Our friendship alone is a risk, and I don't want to be the reason anything bad happens to you," he continued. "I, however, cannot—and will not—stay away. I might have to stop kissing you, but I won't promise to stop seeing you. Do you understand?"

His head snapped to the side, startling me. As I turned to see what he was looking at, I caught small eyes peeping out at me from behind the flower. We both sat quietly, neither of us moving, as a small girl—small enough to fit into the palm of my hand—dashed across the pond and appeared on the table before me.

She moved so quickly that I had a hard time tracking her. Her eyes were the most beautiful shade of bright blue I had ever seen. They took up most of her face, leaving just the perfect amount of room for a mouth and nose.

Her black hair hung to her ankles and covered her body

in the absence of clothes. It floated around her as if she was submerged in water. I smiled as she turned to look at Will and began blushing. My eyes widened as Will chuckled and the little girl moved closer to me, her cheeks turning red.

"It's a forest spirit," Will told me softly. "I've never seen one before. They rarely show themselves like this."

"She's so pretty," I said, and my heart swelled as soft giggles met my ears. I watched as the little girl covered her now-flaming cheeks. "Oh my Goddess!" I didn't move an inch as thin iridescent wings sprouted from her back.

As her wings flapped steadily, her feet lifted off the table and her head tilted to the side as she gazed into my eyes. The smile on my face fell away as an odd feeling of warmth blossomed in my chest. She flew closer to my face, then reached under her hair and pulled out an iridescent flower.

I glanced at Will as she held it out to me, and he nodded. So I opened my hand, and she placed the flower gently in it. She smiled as she held onto a finger and slowly curled it for me to close my hand.

"Thank you," I said to her, and she nodded slowly before flying up into the tree and vanishing.

My heart rate slowly returned to normal, and I opened my palm to examine the flower.

"She blessed you," Will said in shock. "A forest spirit blessed you. Keep that flower. Whisper into it whenever you need help, and you'll receive it." He crossed his arms over his chest. "She didn't give me one."

I laughed. "Jealousy isn't a good look on you. She obviously likes you, so take that and be grateful." I carefully placed the flower in the bosom of my dress. He gave me a strange look. "What?" I asked.

"Nothing." One of his fingers began tapping at his arm. The way he was gazing at me had my stomach clenching. "You keep surprising me, Little Wolf."

"That's what I do best." I picked up my goblet and held it up. No, I didn't want our friendship to end, even if a romance could never happen. "Stay tuned for more."

He held his goblet up as well. "I plan to."

10

ELINOR

onnor stood to the left of the door. Darian, dressed proudly in his black Werewolf Guard uniform, stood to the right. With Connor's blond hair cascading down his shoulders and Darian's curly black hair shaved low at the sides, they looked like the personifications of night and day.

Darian's hazel eyes fell on me, and I narrowed my eyes back at him. I still couldn't stand the guy, and I was sure the feeling was mutual. Sure, I remembered the night I had overheard him talking highly of me to my father. Even so, he'd sabotaged my efforts to join the Guards repeatedly from the first day I expressed interest.

Hater.

"I'm sorry to see you go . . ." My father's voice grabbed my attention, and I looked over to where he and Cyrus were talking.

"It's for the best," Cyrus answered. "After hearing what happened, I knew you'd agree."

I hadn't!

That's what I wanted to yell, and from the look on Skye's

face, she had been hoping for the same—that my father would somehow try to convince Cyrus to stay. A part of me understood that Cyrus leaving was for the best, but as his sister of sorts, it was hard for me to let him go so easily.

Yes, he said he'd return from time to time, but that wasn't enough. To make matters worse, I knew Skye was being ripped apart inside because I, too, would leave soon. My father had only returned a day ago, so we hadn't spoken about my marriage to Elijah just yet. But it was only a matter of time. Or knowing my father, Elijah would just show up one day and that would be when I was finally told what was happening.

"Thank you for saving Elinor and Skye," my father said to Cyrus, placing his fist over his heart. "Our pack will remain open to you always."

"Thank you." Cyrus returned the gesture of respect. "I appreciate everything you've done for me." He nodded to Connor and Darian, who both placed their hands over their hearts as well.

Skye rose from her seat abruptly and barreled out of the room, leaving an awkward silence behind her. My father's knowing eyes darted from the door she had stormed through to Cyrus and then to me.

"I'll speak to her," I told him. "I'll be staying with her tonight after Cyrus leaves."

He nodded. "Before you leave, we have something to talk about. And although Cyrus is leaving, I think he needs to hear it as well." I nodded and sat down where Skye had been. "I'll get straight to it," he said. "Supernaturals and humans were disappearing before this demon appeared. Since the demon Cyrus killed couldn't have been responsible for those disappearances, it would appear we still have an issue on our hands."

"What? Disappearing how?" Darian asked as his thick, dark brows pulled together. Considering he was a Werewolf Guard and obviously just hearing about this now, I could understand the look of shock and anger in his eyes.

I had been right, then. After Cyrus had killed the demon, I'd had a horrible feeling that things weren't about to miraculously get better.

"How long has this been going on?" Darian asked my father.

"A few months, from what I've been told. But it's been steadily getting worse. Two more people went missing in the last week—a human and an elf. So the leaders of the various races have finally agreed to make this public. They were waiting until we caught whoever was responsible for the recent deaths, just in case the killer was the same. But since that's been solved and people are still going missing—"

"Now it's time to put others on alert," Connor interjected, and my father nodded.

My father's eyes darted back and forth rapidly, a thoughtful expression on his face. "We still know very little about what's going on. So far, there's been limited evidence to go on. But it's becoming too much of an issue now, so . . ." He looked at Darian. "Notify your Guards to keep an eye out." Then he turned to Connor. "Double the patrols around the pack both night and day."

"Yes, Alpha," both men said in unison before turning and leaving.

"Cyrus?" Cyrus stood up as my father said his name.

"Since you'll be leaving, could you keep an eye out and let me know if you see or hear anything?"

"Yes, of course, Alpha," Cyrus answered without hesitation.

"Good, thank you. Now, if you don't mind, I'd like to have a minute with my daughter."

I frowned at that but watched as Cyrus left before I turned to my father. I hoped against hope that he'd changed his mind.

"Elijah will arrive within the week. I'm waiting for his confirmation. Are you ready?" he asked.

I clenched my jaw for a moment as my mind took me back to the magical date I shared with Will. "As ready as I'll ever be."

When I stood up to leave, he rose and held his hand out to stop me. "Elinor." I turned to him, an awkward tension sizzling between us. "I know things between us haven't been what they should be, but I want you to know that everything I do, even if you don't approve of it, is to keep you safe."

And that, right there, was my problem.

"There are other ways to keep me safe, Father." I went to leave, but as I walked forward, the office door opened, and my mother and Jackson walked in.

"Sister!" Jackson yelled, and I couldn't help smiling. "Look, I made this for you. Mother said you're leaving soon, so I want you to have a drawing of all of us."

I took the brown paper from him. I grinned at the paint slashed across it that created two figures standing to the left of the paper and another two to the right at the top.

"That's you and me at the front, and Mother and Father at

the back," Jackson explained, and across the room, our father growled.

"Why am I not in front?" he asked as his lips curved into a grin.

Jackson shook his head. "Elinor and I are in front because you're old now."

Our mother erupted with laughter while our father gasped in mock horror. "Thank you, I'll cherish this always," I said to my brother.

"Good, because it was hard to draw," Jackson added with a pout. "I wish you didn't have to leave."

My parents' laughter died away, and an uncomfortable silence filled the room. I avoided looking at either of them, but I kissed Jackson on the cheek. "I'll come back and see you," I told him. "So don't worry about that. I'm not leaving forever. I'll put this in my room so I don't forget it, okay?"

He nodded, causing his curls to bounce.

"Mom, I'm staying over at Skye's tonight, okay?" I called out.

"Okay, honey," she replied, and I quickly left the room.

I wish I wasn't leaving either, Jackson. More than you'll ever know.

Elinor

Cyrus and I left together, planning to go to Skye's house. She'd been home for a while already after leaving my father's office earlier we did.

Cyrus sighed. "She's pissed."

"Yeah, I feel like crap," I grumbled, but Cyrus shook his head.

"You shouldn't. You don't have a choice in leaving. But I'm voluntarily leaving the pack. I mean, sure, I'm doing it to protect her and everyone here, but still, I'm choosing to leave." We descended the stairs together, making our way to the first floor. "She's angrier at me than at you."

"Even so, I feel horrible. And yeah, I'm mad at you, too."

"Sorry," he said, chuckling as we made our way outside. "You two don't have to do this, you know. I don't need a party."

"It'll just be the three of us. Skye's mother has already decided to cook a massive dinner, so you're staying for the night." I rolled my eyes. "Well, you're leaving tonight, but not until late. Since you're so proud of those wings of yours, Skye and I will eventually let you fly away . . . after we finish with you."

Elinor

"Dinner was great, Ms. Clementine." Skye's mother blushed at Cyrus's compliment as she cleared the table.

"Thank you, Cyrus." Her hazel eyes, so much like Skye's, grew sad. "I'm just sorry to see you go. You're like a son to me. I mean, you've always had your freedom to come and go, but this is different." My eyes slid to Skye, who was looking away, trying to hide her teary eyes. "Oh no." Ms. Clementine held her hand up as Cyrus went to help her clear the table. "I'll do it."

We all sat in silence as Skye's mother washed the dishes, but Cyrus couldn't stop himself from offering to dry them. "Please, let me do something before I leave."

While Skye's hair was dark and curly and fell to her shoulders, her mother's hair was dark brown with loose curls that went to the middle of her back. She stared up at Cyrus for a moment, her face growing even sadder, then she suddenly pulled him into a hug.

"Take care of yourself, okay?" she whispered as she released him and stepped back. My emotions started to get the better of me as she cupped his cheek. "Come back to visit soon, all right? I think I'm going to turn in early tonight."

"I will, I promise," Cyrus reassured her, and she patted his chest before turning away.

"Goodnight, Ms. Clementine," I told her as she walked by the table and kissed Skye on her head. Then she smiled at me, flashing her pearly white teeth. "Goodnight, honey."

After she left the room, we sat in silence. Cyrus and I shared a look as Skye reclined in her chair with her eyes trained on the table. I bit down on my lip, unsure of what to say. I shared Skye's disappointment that our best friend was leaving, but for her, it was more than that. The man she loved was going away.

She cried so hard when she told me about Cyrus only having three years left on Earth. I hadn't been able to stop myself from comparing it to the somewhat similar situation Will and I were facing. Only I was the one who would leave while he refused to even contemplate an end to this thing between us.

I recalled the words he had said to me—that no matter what, we'd remain friends—and smiled. I closed my eyes as I went to the dragon forest in my mind. Taking me to such a magical place was one of the greatest gifts anyone had ever given me. I would now have such a calming memory to return to in the future.

"What are you smiling at?" Skye asked, and my eyes flew open.

"Oh, just remembering something," I told her. "So does this mean you're talking again? Whenever you get quiet, it's kind of scary."

She looked at Cyrus. "I guess. This is just how things have to be, I suppose."

"I really am sorry," Cyrus said as he sat down again, this time closer to Skye.

She smiled at him sadly. "I know, and don't be. You're doing this to keep us safe."

Cyrus lifted his hand as if to touch her cheek, then pulled his hand away and looked my way.

I rolled my eyes. It was cute that they were trying to not be too lovey-dovey with each other around me, but honestly, I loved seeing them like this. I had endured the fools not noticing their mutual feelings for years. "Oh no, don't hold back on my account." I looked in the direction Skye's mother had gone. "But aren't you guys worried that—"

"She knows," Skye blurted, looking in the same direction I was. "She overheard Cyrus and me talking the other day. But she said she knew all along that we had feelings for each other."

"Yeah, I think most people around here have noticed that.

You two are the slow ones." I laughed as Skye rolled her eyes. "But, um, there's something I need to tell you guys."

I reached into my bosom and pulled out the flower the forest spirit had given me. Skye leaned forward to get a closer look, and the iridescent flower sparkled.

"Where did you get that?" Cyrus asked as he, too, leaned in for a better view.

"Do you know what it is?" I held my hand out to him and he shook his head. "I got it from Dragon Territory."

Skye frowned. "Excuse me? When did you venture into Dragon Territory, and how? There aren't even any close to here."

"Will took you, didn't he?" Cyrus reclined in his seat as Skye looked at him and then at me.

Cyrus's facial expression was unreadable, but Skye's face immediately lit up with excitement at the mention of Will taking me somewhere. "Is that true? Will took you to see a Dragon Territory? But how? What was it like? Did you see a dragon?"

I nodded as excitement bubbled within me at the memory. "I spoke to one. She was stunning, and she could transform into a human-like form." I closed my eyes for a moment. "The forest was so colorful and filled with creatures we've never even imagined. Because dragons are spiritual creatures, their territories overflow with energy. And since they are so reclusive, that energy doesn't get tainted by outsiders, you know?" I opened my eyes and looked down at the flower in my hand. "A forest spirit gave this to me—a girl who was smaller than my hand."

Skye held her hand out, and I gently slid the flower into her palm. Her brows knitted. "It's warm."

"Yeah, I noticed that, too. I figure it's alive. Will said that if I'm ever in trouble, I can whisper into it asking for help, and I'll get it."

Cyrus's mouth turned downward. "Well, I guess it's a good thing to have. But for a spirit to give that to you, she must have sensed something special about you. Maybe that you're a firstblood and strong?"

Skye gave the flower back to me, and I returned it to my bosom. "Yeah, maybe."

I decided not to tell them about what had happened with the weeping willow tree, which I still had no explanation for. Seeing the look on Cyrus's face, I could tell he wasn't too fond of this conversation. I didn't blame him for not trusting Will, but my feelings for him had only grown stronger after our date.

Will and I spent hours alone together in the dragon forest before finally returning back home. I placed my elbow on the table, recalling my father's words that Elijah would arrive soon. Then, I thought about Will and I kissing each other goodbye after our date was over—even after I had promised myself that I wouldn't let things go that far again.

I shook my head and closed my eyes while Skye and Cyrus chatted. When had I become so attached to Will? I began mentally searching through the moments we'd spent together before our date, but I couldn't tell exactly when I became so enthralled by him.

Loyalty was very important to me, but I knew I'd still want Will even after marrying Elijah—no matter how hard I tried not to. A mating bond would have removed all the feelings I had for him, but my marriage to Elijah wasn't a mated match. Sure, we might learn to love each other, but how long would that take?

What's wrong with me?

Werewolves and vampires were enemies. Who knew what would happen if anyone ever discovered our complicated and highly taboo relationship? Still, Will refused to stay away from me. And I still enjoyed being with him. A part of me genuinely didn't care if my father found out about us. Sure, the initial disgrace would turn my world upside down and he'd no doubt try to hunt Will down to kill him, but . . . not even the risk of that happening could make me walk away from Will.

A tear slipped from my eye, and Skye and Cyrus fell silent as I raised my hand to wipe the tear away.

Why does this all have to be so complicated?

"Elinor?" Skye placed her hand over mine, and my other hand fell away from my face. "Elinor, what's wrong?"

"What is wrong with me?" I asked her. "I-I feel like I'm standing on the sideline, watching everything in my life change without having any say in it. Will and I aren't like you two. Our friendship is forbidden. There is no accepting anything between us, not from his kind and not from mine. Werewolves hunt and kill his people." I wiped at another tear. "I'm going against everything I would have stood for as a Guard by being his friend, but . . . he's not a monster. I mean, I'm not naïve—he still has to feed, and I know he's taken lives, but—" I covered my face and sighed.

"But I still care about him. I don't feel like the female firstborn of an Alpha when I'm with him. I just feel like me, Elinor, without the weight of my family name." I wiped my face and inhaled deeply as I fixated on a small ant walking across the table. "Elijah doesn't want me, and I don't want him. What kind of marriage are we going to have when we both have feelings for someone else? At least Will and I aren't officially together, but the humiliation Elijah's girlfriend—or ex-girlfriend—will have to deal with every day after I marry him? I can't even imagine."

My face scrunched up as another thought occurred to me—something I'd thought about in the past. "And what happens if he meets his mate after we're married?" I looked from Cyrus to Skye. "What if I do? My dilemma with Will would come to an end, but what would happen to my marriage?"

I exhaled heavily as I slumped down in my chair. I felt lighter after getting all that off my chest. Nothing was solved, but finally voicing my thoughts and feelings felt good.

Suddenly, I realized just what I'd said. "I, um, I just meant that I feel comfortable around Will. It's not like I'm in love with him or anything. We just . . . get along, you know? And for some reason, I just . . . I don't want to lose that. I mean—"

"We understand, Elinor—maybe more than anyone else ever could," Cyrus said, looking at Skye.

"That won't be on you or Elijah if either of you finds your mate. You were both forced into it," Skye argued.

"I'm not going to do it," I said through clenched teeth. "I won't marry Elijah. And not just because of Will, but because it's not right. Then all I have to do is to stop seeing Will, and that problem will be solved, too."

"Stop downplaying your feelings," Cyrus suddenly growled as he interlocked his fingers on the table. "I saw him kiss you. You like Will, and that's fine. You can't control who you end up liking sometimes." He looked at Skye, and she blushed as he reached out and took her hand. "Sure, occasionally the person you end up falling for will only bring about judgment, but in the end, you just have to put your happiness first."

He kissed the back of Skye's hand, and I smiled. Cyrus left his family behind without caring what any of them would think of him and had remained on Earth, where he was happy. He'd done what he felt was right for him. He and Skye loved each other, and neither of them seemed to care about someone discovering their romance and judging them for it anymore. And because of Cyrus's affiliation with the pack, their relationship was more likely to be accepted by some.

I didn't have those options. Sure, I'd do what was right regarding my proposed marriage to Elijah, but as for Will, all I could do was accept my feelings for him. We might never be able to hold hands in public like Skye and Cyrus, but the stress I'd placed on myself by trying to hold back my feelings would be over.

"Wait, Cyrus! You basically just told Skye you love her, that you've fallen for her. Am I missing something here?" I pointed at them both. "Did you guys profess your love already or something? I mean, I know about the feeding." Skye slapped my arm hard, the sound echoing through the room. "Oops, sorry! Goddess, that hurt!" I whispered. "But have the words 'I love you' been said?"

Skye pulled her hand away from Cyrus as she growled, "Stop! You're making it weird."

"Oh my Goddess, you guys are so cute!" I leaned forward so only they could hear, just in case Skye's mother wasn't sleeping. "So, have you had sex yet?" I dodged Skye's punch and got up quickly. "Hey, I had to ask. You two have been skimpy on the details."

"Well, now you know how it feels. We're always hearing stuff from you two or three days after it's already happened," Skye countered. "Visiting a Dragon Territory and only just telling us now." She shook her head.

I hunched my shoulders sheepishly and grinned. "Sorry?" I returned to the table and held my hand out to her. Then I reached out my other hand to Cyrus, who took it immediately. Skye slipped her hand into mine and then held hands with Cyrus. "I love you guys, and I know we're about to split apart for the first time in our lives, but . . ." I squeezed Cyrus's hand as he smiled. "Nothing will keep us apart forever, and that includes you going back to the Underworld," I said, nodding to him. "There has to be some way to see you or speak to you. But we'll figure that out when the time comes."

He kissed the back of my hand and then Skye's. "I love you both, and I thank you for the life you helped me to build here. Truly." Then he stood up and my face fell, as did Skye's. "I should get going."

"No," Skye whimpered. "Can't you stay a little longer?"

"Why can't you just stay until morning?" I added.

He bit his bottom lip as he looked towards the window. "I'd rather fly through the night. Since I'll be traveling to a place I've never visited before, I'd like to avoid the added attention my wings tend to bring."

I sighed and stood up, my chair scraping against the floor. "All right." I walked around the table, and he pulled me into a hug. Biting down on my lip, I tried to hold back my tears. "I'd better be seeing you soon, or I'm coming after you."

"I know," he laughed as I released him and stepped back.

"I, um, I'm going to head upstairs," I said. He nodded, then glanced at Skye as I turned away.

"I feel like I'm losing you," I heard Skye say as I closed her bedroom door. "Seeing you only now and then won't be enough for me."

I know how you feel, Skye. I know how you feel.

11

ELINOR

I moaned in protest as the sound of heavy breathing pulled me from my slumber. I snuggled further into my pillow, but the sound didn't stop, forcing me to roll onto my back.

Eyes closed, I reached out with my arm to nudge Skye to get her to stop whatever she was doing, but the spot beside me on the bed was empty and cold. That's when I noticed a rhythmic thump of a third heartbeat within the room. My eyes popped open and my body instantly tensed when I glimpsed a figure standing on the other side of the room.

A bulky black cloak fully covered its body, the voluminous hood completely obscuring its face. Behind the figure, light from a swirling purple portal filled the room. But what had me panicking was the sight of Skye suspended in the air, her eyes wide with terror.

She had been breathing loudly to wake me up, but the seconds I'd spent in shock trying to understand what was happening had wasted too much time. For a second, my heart stopped beating as her eyes closed and she fell unconscious. I was utterly confused about what was happening—my mind was still foggy with sleep—but that wouldn't stop me from saving Skye.

"Sk—" I tried to scream but choked with her name lodged in my throat as I levitated off the bed. Everything was happening so quickly. And I couldn't detect a scent from the cloaked figure.

What the hell's going on?

I tried to move but couldn't. I continued to float upward towards the ceiling. It felt as if something had suddenly grabbed my body and was moving me in any direction it wished. That only pissed me off further, but the power surrounding me tightened, and I abruptly felt sleepy.

I closed my eyes for a moment as I inhaled deeply. Skye and I were about to be taken, and there was no way I could let that happen. I was Elinor Blackwood, firstborn daughter of an Alpha. I had no intention of letting some creep sneak into my territory and kidnap me!

I opened my eyes and called on my wolf, forcing my rage and power to flood the room as I released a thundering howl. The figure stepped back as if frightened, and I was released in seconds, falling back onto the bed. I was immediately on my feet as Skye's body floated towards the figure more quickly.

The mysterious hooded figure had no doubt planned on keeping us suspended in the air until we were both unconscious before taking us.

"Put her down immediately, or I'm going to strangle you with that hideous cloak!" I shouted as I hunched forward, my eyes turning black. But all I got was a masculine chuckle in response.

So it's a male.

I looked towards the room door, wondering why Ms. Clementine hadn't woken up. Surely, she could hear what was going on. I had howled loud enough for wolves patrolling the forest to hear.

I turned my attention back to the cloaked figure. "Okay, then. I'll teach you not to piss off an Alpha-born!"

I rushed forward to attack but smacked directly into some sort of invisible barrier. I slammed my hand against it as my claws pierced through my fingertips. I curled my fingers against the barrier and started pushing, digging my fingers through the invisible wall that was pushing me back.

Groaning loudly, I tried to break through, my heartbeat spiking as my groans turned to howls. Veins appeared on my hands as the space in front of them shimmered. On the other side, the cloaked figure stood motionless, as if surprised I was fighting back—or intrigued that I was.

This was the guy's chance to escape with Skye, but he was just standing there. My jaw clenched as I channeled all my strength into my hands, and my claws finally pierced the barrier.

That's when the man finally moved. My eyes widened with panic as he stepped through the barrier and vanished. For a split second, I thought he was giving up and leaving, but I was wrong.

I leaped into the air as Skye's body floated above me towards the portal. "No!"

My fingers were inches away from her arm when a dagger came flying through the portal, embedding itself in my side. The force of it threw me across the room and into the wall above the bed, which broke under my weight as I fell onto it.

The pain was excruciating, but my eyes remained on Skye as I watched her slip into the portal. "No!"

I was back on my feet within seconds, wincing from the pain spreading across my side to my back and across my stomach. I tried to ignore it as I ran forward, my eyes blurring with tears, but when I reached out to grab Skye's hand—the only part of her not yet engulfed by the portal—another dagger came flying towards me. The blade only nicked my cheek but caused me to falter. A second later and it would have pierced my face.

I fell to the ground as the portal disappeared with Skye—with my best friend—and the room plunged back into darkness.

I started shaking as I pressed a hand to my side to slow the blood loss. Blood from my cheek dripped onto the floor as my eyes darted around the room with confusion. That's when I recalled my father telling us about the recent disappearances of other supernaturals.

No.

I closed my eyes in realization as they burned with tears. "No," I said through clenched teeth. "Not Skye, not Skye, please, Goddess, not her."

I inhaled deeply as I got to my feet. There was no scent left behind. It was as if nobody had been in the room. Even Skye's scent had vanished. Still shaking, I ran from the room, my clothes ripping as I shifted mid-stride.

I checked Ms. Clementine's room. My chest grew weak when I found it empty and devoid of her scent. I backed out of the room, trying not to panic. I rushed from the house, my legs carrying me quickly through the forest.

I have to warn Father!

Alpha Grayson

Elinor's pained howl echoed in my ear, and I bolted upright in bed. For a moment, I thought I had only imagined the howl. But it came again in a second, echoing through the woods, and all traces of sleep left me. I sprang out of bed and jumped through the window on the second floor to land outside.

Something's wrong!

I spotted Elinor's white wolf charging through the forest, and her mother landed on her feet by my side a second later. "Grayson, what's going on?"

Without even knowing what was happening, Clarice had followed me. I smiled on the inside as we both started running towards our daughter. "I don't know." I inhaled deeply and the smell of Elinor's blood had my wolf immediately pushing to the forefront. "She's hurt!" I picked up the pace as Elinor stopped running and began shifting back into her human form. "Elinor, what's going on?"

Her face was slick with tears, her eyes wide as blood ran down her cheek to her neck. "S-Skye, s-she . . . I-I couldn't . . ."

She wasn't making any sense, and my wolf lost control at the sight of all the blood running down her side and right leg.

"Elinor, ground yourself! What happened?"

"S-someone took Skye! Someone took her! They pulled her into a portal and took her! I went looking for Ms. Clementine after I couldn't save Skye, and she was gone as well!" She leaned forward, her face twisting with pain as she grabbed her side. "He took them!"

Connor appeared along with Darian and a few other wolves who were on patrol at night. "What's going on?" Connor asked as his eyes anxiously looked Elinor up and down.

He'd always treated her like a little sister in the same way I'd treated him like a son, and the anger on his face at her wounds reflected that. But it was nothing compared to the fury I was feeling. As Alpha, I was trying to remain calm, but seeing my daughter standing before me covered in blood and tears nearly did me in. This was what I'd tried so hard to avoid.

"Tell me what happened, baby!" My need to rip whoever had done this apart was worsening by the minute. "Who did this?"

"We have to get her back!" Elinor screamed. Her face was red, her black eyes frantic, and she turned around as if to run back into the forest as she began shifting. Her right shoulder dislocated, and another scream tore from her lips. "We have to get her back!" she said loudly, and her mother wrapped her arms around her.

"Don't shift!" she told her, but Elinor was barely listening as she shook her head. "You're wounded and not thinking clearly!"

"She's losing too much blood!" Darian yelled. I moved my Luna aside so I could pick Elinor up. I held her close as she tried to get away, but with the amount of blood she had lost, she was too weak to put up much of a fight.

"It must have been the kidnappers—the ones who are responsible for all those disappearances you told us about, Alpha. Who else would dare attack our pack like this?" Connor voiced as we all ran back to the house.

Those bastards were on my territory—they'd attacked my pack! And they'd taken two of my people! My wolf's need for vengeance had me fighting back against the urge to shift. I was seething at the violation and the disrespect of someone daring to harm *my* daughter. But seeing her healed was my priority right now.

"Darian, Connor, start searching now! Find out if anyone else is missing and track Skye's scent. Don't come back until you've found her!"

"Yes, Alpha!"

Elinor

The pungent smell of herbs had my nose scrunching up as I opened my eyes. I looked down at my side to find a bandage wrapped around my stomach, and I bolted upright as my memories returned.

"Skye," I whispered under my breath as I ripped the bandage off and inspected my wound, almost fully healed now. I got dressed quickly and began making my way downstairs.

I hadn't been able to save her. I hadn't been able to protect her! What good was I, an Alpha-born with incredible strength, if I couldn't even save my best friend? Sure, the kidnapper had caught me off guard, but still . . . After meeting Will, I'd realized how much there still was for me to learn about the world, about other supernaturals . . . about magic. The vampires I fought the night I'd met Will and during the Werewolf Guard examination were child's play in comparison to some of the dangerous creatures I now knew existed. Yet, at the time, I thought I was showcasing true strength and power.

I had been useless in the fight against the demon who had been sent after Cyrus, and now I wasn't strong enough or fast enough to save Skye from her abductors.

I shook my head as I made my way to the first floor. This wasn't the time for self-pity, and I was not a weakling! Of course, I had more to learn—so much more—and, of course, there were other beings that had the strength to beat my ass. Still, whoever had taken Skye was going to feel my wrath— no matter how much power they had!

I followed the sound of voices and found Darian, Connor, and my father in the living room. "Did you find her?"

They fell silent.

"Elinor, you should rest," Connor said.

I clenched my fists. "Do you want me to pull my dress up and show you my healed wound? I'm fine. Now, where is she?"

"Her scent disappeared, Elinor," my father said, and the only pinch of hope I had left vanished. "We went to her house, but we couldn't find her scent anywhere in the house. We have no way of tracking her or her mother."

"How is it even possible to completely erase someone's scent? It couldn't have faded naturally so quickly," I argued as

I grew frantic at how calm they all appeared. "There has to be something we can do!" I turned to Darian. "You're a Guard! Can't you find her?"

"I sent Guards out to try to pick up on her scent, but so far, there's nothing. We're doing everything we can, Elinor." Darian's hazel eyes darkened for a moment. "We want her back, too."

I said nothing as I stared out the window. It sickened me that today was so beautiful and bright . . . and painfully sad. I shook my head as I covered my face with my hands. I understood everyone was angry—it wasn't just me—and as the Alpha, my father had to be more concerned than ever about his pack. Still, I couldn't just sit around and do nothing.

The pain of feeling useless would be the end of me. I couldn't stay inside this house while Skye and Ms. Clementine were out there somewhere.

I turned around to leave, but my father noticed. "Elinor, I think it's best if you remain here at the packhouse."

"Father, I need air. Okay? I have to go out."

I turned and left, dawdling as I made my way into the forest. I gritted my teeth as the memories of what had happened last night kept replaying in my mind, taunting me. As much as I tried to remember any useful detail I might have missed while fighting, there was nothing. Whoever that cloaked person was, he had been careful. He had touched nothing—he hadn't needed to. All he'd had to do was float Skye and me into his portal.

He hadn't even had a scent. If it hadn't been for Skye's loud breathing, I probably wouldn't have woken up at all.

As I walked, I rubbed my hand across my forehead in exasperation. Maybe if Cyrus had stayed until the morning, none of this would have happened. He could have saved Skye and captured the guy who took her. I looked down at my hands, watching my claws elongate.

Stronger, I need to get stronger.

I gritted my teeth as I growled and swiped my claws at a tree, shredding its trunk and causing it to fall.

I need to get Skye back!

My chest tightened as my emotions bubbled over. "I'm *so* sorry." First, I'd failed Meeka during the Werewolf Guard examination. I had been too weak and couldn't do as she wished—couldn't kill her before she changed into a vampire. And now I wasn't strong enough to save Skye when she needed me most. I shook my head and walked away to press my forehead to another tree. "I'll make things right, I swear. Just hold on, Skye. There has to be a way to track you down."

"Elinor!" I spun around as Ione screamed my name. She was waving and running breathlessly towards me. I wondered how far I'd wandered into the forest for her to appear so tired. "There is a way."

My heart skipped a beat. "What are you talking about?" I hurried towards her, quickly grabbing her arm as she swayed. She was almost wheezing now, and blood was running from her nose. "Ione, what the hell? What's wrong? You're bleeding."

She wiped away the blood with the back of her hand. "Skye was like a big sister to me. She-she still is, I mean." She closed her eyes for a moment and swallowed hard. "There is a way to save her. I mind-linked with Cyrus."

"What?" I yelled. "You're not experienced enough to mind-link, Ione. You could have—"

"Please, Elinor, just don't. I don't need a lecture. Cyrus is the only one who can track her down. He's a demon. As powerful as werewolves are, we're useless without a scent to track. We need more information than we have now, which is nothing."

I stared at the fourteen-year-old girl in shock. Ione had always been wise beyond her years, but I'd never seen this side of her before. No wonder she was exhausted. Connecting to another person's mind took years of practice.

"You spoke to Cyrus, then?" I asked, and she nodded.

"It was the first time I've ever done a mind-link, so all I could say was that he needed to come back and save Skye before the link ended." Her blue eyes shone with determination. "I hope it was enough."

I squeezed her shoulder. "As reckless as it was, I'm sure your message will be enough."

"You do reckless stuff all the time." She grinned. Then her face paled, and she started coughing up blood.

"Damn it, we need to get you to your mother."

A chill appeared in the air, along with a darkness I was now familiar with. As I looked up towards the sky, something flew over our heads. The power behind Cyrus's wings had the trees swaying wildly.

"Cyrus!" I yelled. In seconds, he returned, landing with so much force that the earth beneath his feet cracked.

His eyes were red as he walked towards me, the faintest cloud of black smoke rising from his body. "Where is she? What's going on?"

"A guy in a cloak abducted Skye." I wasn't surprised he had returned so quickly. Cyrus would do anything for Skye. "They took Ms. Clementine as well. We think it was the person or people who have been abducting mortals and supernaturals alike. But no one else from the pack was taken." I looked down at the girl beside me. The bleeding was getting worse. "But we need to take Ione back to her mother first."

"I'll take her home." Cyrus walked over and picked Ione up. His wings flapped once as he pushed off the ground to hover above me. "Meet me at Skye's house."

I nodded. "Got it."

Then he flew up through the trees and disappeared. Quickly I began removing my dress, revealing the uniform given to me during my Werewolf Guard examination. Now that Cyrus was back, I knew there was no way he was going to sit around and do nothing. And I wasn't going to let him search for Skye alone.

I shifted into my wolf and watched as my pants and top liquefied and slipped into the ring on my finger. It seemed as if I made the right choice in keeping this uniform.

Hang on, Skye. We're coming.

12

CYRUS

I sat down on Skye's bed with my eyes closed, trying to remain calm. Someone took my Skye—that was a fact. And now, every second would count until I got her back. I opened my eyes slowly as I inhaled and clenched my fist. Her scent was completely gone from the room. Smells faded over time, but not this quickly. I'd been inside this house with Skye and her mother just hours ago, and now it was like they'd never even lived here.

As easy as it would be to lose my shit, that wouldn't help either of them. Ms. Clementine had accepted me from the moment I had arrived. She'd raised me, cared for me, and never once made me feel unwelcome. And I wouldn't rest until I'd returned both her and her daughter back home.

Ione had drained her energy almost completely from doing that mind-link, but I'd be forever grateful.

I heard Elinor open the front door and sprint through the house to Skye's room. Her eyes fell on me and her shoulders immediately slumped. Her eyes became glossy, and I stood up and pulled her into a hug.

"She was right there, Cyrus." She pointed across the room. "I could have saved her."

"Shh, don't do that, Elinor. Nurse Hilary told me about your wounds. If you blame yourself, then I would have to blame myself as well, and that won't help anything. I could have stayed one more night as you both had asked. But I didn't, and someone snatched her. We can't change that. I know you must have done everything you could to save her, but right now we need to focus on getting her back."

I stepped back, and her face grew serious as she nodded. Her eyes fell on the wall across the room, and her brow arched at the large hole. She took my bruised hand in hers and squeezed it.

"We'll get them back," she whispered. "We just have to figure out how. We know nothing about what's going on, and now we don't even have Skye's smell to track. Have you ever heard of a person's scent being completely removed like this?"

I shook my head. "I've heard of potions that can hide your scent, but I've never heard of something like this before. But clearly, it's not impossible." As I walked over to the window, I picked up Skye's hairbrush from where it rested on her chair. As I realized what I had to do, I sighed.

"I'll get her back." I turned to face Elinor, who was eyeing me curiously.

"Okay, I'm coming with you."

I knew that was what she'd want to do the moment I saw what she was wearing. Her Werewolf Guard examination uniform would allow her to shift and return to human form without losing her clothing. It would come in handy, but even so, there was no way in hell I was allowing her to come with me.

"Cyrus, I wasn't asking permission, so don't push me on this. I promise you now, I'll lose my shit. And you know damn well I'll follow you." She pointed to the brush in my hand. "What are you going to do?"

I looked down at the brush that still had strands of Skye's dark hair in it. "Something I wish I didn't have to do. I really can't take you with me, Elinor."

Her eyes changed to black as she walked toward me and pointed her finger at my face. "How about we don't waste time arguing about this? I'm coming. I might not have been able to save her from being abducted right in front of me, but I'll be damned if I don't do everything I can to get her back."

"Aren't you forgetting something? They could have killed you, Elinor! Your father isn't going to let you go with me, and you know that."

She inhaled and closed her eyes. When she opened them, she said, "And let me remind you that I'm not a child. I have no intention of asking him if I can go. So . . . I think that solves that. I'll deal with his anger after we return with Skye and Ms. Clementine."

We stared each other down for a few minutes until I shook my head and walked around her. She was right. Arguing with her was wasting valuable time. Where I'd be going was dangerous—even for me—but knowing Elinor, she really would follow me if I left without her.

And I totally understood how she felt. It was taking all my strength not to punch myself. If only I had stayed until morning! I balled my hands into fists, allowing my nails to press into my flesh to stop myself from thinking about what might happen to Skye and Ms. Clementine.

I can't lose her.

Shaking my head, I exited the house at the rear and changed back into my demon form. Where we'd be going would take us days by foot but less than twenty-four hours if I flew straight without stopping. Carrying Elinor would slow me down, but the faster we left, the quicker we'd get there.

I turned to Elinor to tell her to get on my back and caught her staring at the bench I made for Skye a few months ago. Whenever I wasn't traveling or visiting the Demon Realm, the three of us spent hours chatting and laughing together on that bench. I realized then that there were many spots that were special to us—like the tree in the forest where I had saved Skye from a Bleeder. My heart felt as if someone was holding it in their hand and squeezing it . . . I shook my head. I didn't want to think like this . . . like Skye was never coming back.

"We need to go," I whispered to Elinor, and she nodded.

My wings emerged from my back, and Elinor climbed on. Then we took to the sky. The night was chilly and the stars bright, the perfect night to gaze at the heavens with the woman I loved. If only she were here . . .

"The place we're going, you're going to see things—awful things. Don't react in your usual way, okay?"

Elinor placed her chin on my shoulder. "What usual way?"

"Don't start a fight. Just ignore the things you'll see and let me do the talking, okay?"

"I'm not an animal, I can control myself. But where are

we going? Are we going to the Demon Realm or something?" she asked loudly, trying to be heard above the strong winds.

"No. Just don't talk to anyone."

Elinor wouldn't be the only one who would have to face her father's wrath when we returned—not when I was the one who allowed her to come with me. Especially if she got hurt in the process of saving Skye. But if their roles were reversed, I knew Skye would do the same thing for her. How could I be the one to hold her back?

Thunder rumbled around us, and Elinor sighed. "Great, just what we need right now. So, how long do you think it'll take for my father and the others to realize I left?"

I shrugged as I felt the first drop of water on my shoulder. "Not long, but after this rain, I doubt they'll be able to track our scent. Sorry for not asking earlier, but how's your side?"

"It's fine," she answered. "It healed pretty quickly. The two daggers that he threw didn't have any scent on them either. Surprise, surprise."

I hummed my response, and we flew on in silence as the rain started in earnest. Skye's hazel eyes flashed in my mind, and I quickly dipped to the side as a lightning bolt flashed right by us.

"Can you watch where you're flying? I'm flammable, and that bolt was a little too close for comfort."

Elinor

s Cyrus lowered me to the ground, I bent backward and groaned as my back popped. Then I leaned forward and touched my toes to loosen my stiff muscles. We had flown throughout the night but were forced to stop for an hour in the morning because of the storm. Finally, after what felt like an eternity of flying again, Cyrus descended.

I turned in a circle after properly stretching and frowned. "W-where are we?" All around us, for as far as I could see, was a wasteland of sand. "Are we lost?" Even though it was evening, the heat rising from the ground was almost unbearable.

"We're in Kurto, the Land of Whispers. Listen," he said. I stood still, and in a few seconds, I could hear the faint whispers in the wind.

"What's making the sounds, though? I don't hear any heartbeats."

"Snakes," he answered, and I immediately looked down. "Sometimes they are louder, tricking travelers into thinking someone needs help." He started walking. "Stay close to me."

He didn't have to tell me twice. I followed his every step. "Yeah, I'm not interested in being bitten by a snake."

Despite my trepidation about the snakes, I was beyond excited. I'd spent very little time beyond the boundaries of my pack, so I knew very little about the world. As dangerous as this wasteland might be, I couldn't help being a little intrigued about the kind of creatures that might live in such a hot place.

"Look," Cyrus said, pointing to our left. My mouth

dropped as I watched the sand a few meters away from us begin to move.

"Cyrus, is that a snake?" He nodded, and I shook my head. This was unbelievable. Even though it was beneath the sand, I could tell that it was at least thirty-two feet long. "That's huge! You didn't tell me these snakes could swallow me whole." He shrugged as if he didn't really care, and we kept walking.

We continued on for about thirty minutes, and I tried my best not to ask any more questions about where we were going. But I simply couldn't hold it in any longer.

"So, will we be there soon?"

"Yeah, in a few more minutes. Have you ever heard of the Black Souls Market?" He stopped and turned to me. "I'm guessing from the look on your face that the answer is yes. If I'd told you our destination earlier, would you have still come with me?"

"I still would have come with you. But the Black Souls Market is avoided for a reason. It's like a playground for dark creatures, and supernaturals are sold there." I shivered a little, then tilted my head to the side. "The market is always moving. How did you know where to find it?"

He didn't answer me, just started walking again. Cyrus was always leaving the pack and venturing off somewhere, so I really shouldn't have been surprised that he knew his way around here. But because of the wicked things that went on in the market, it wasn't somewhere I ever thought he'd go. He was a demon, sure, but . . . he was Cyrus.

"I found the market when I first got my cravings," he answered hesitantly a few minutes later. He cracked his knuckles as a crease appeared between his brows. "It's where I learned to control my hunger."

There was a haunted look on his face as he scrutinized the area. I had noticed his demeanor change—become more brooding—the longer we had flown. It was as if the closer we got to our destination, the more his dark powers became noticeable. He hadn't talked about that time in his life with Skye or me, not even once. And now I understood why. The horrible stories I'd heard about the market were fodder for nightmares.

"Oh," I muttered.

He removed my cloak from the bag he was carrying and handed it to me. "Put your cloak on and pull your hood far over your face. And no matter what you do, don't shift. Stories about white wolves are known in the market. I'd rather not have you become a target."

"Yeah, I understand," I said as I did what he asked. Then he held his hand out, and the space just beyond it shimmered.

He held his other hand out to me. "Ready?" I nodded. "Good. Stay close to me."

He pushed his hand through the barrier, and it vanished. I inhaled deeply to ground myself and called on my wolf to further heighten my senses. I'd need to remain on alert.

We stepped through the barrier, and the sensation of it on my face felt like slime from a snail. But once we stepped out on the other side, the sudden transition from day to night was the least shocking thing I saw.

Cyrus pulled his hood over his head as a cocktail of screams echoed around us. "Welcome to Black Souls Market."

13

ELINOR

The air was thicker than it had been moments ago. The darkness that lingered in the Black Souls Market felt dense and unnatural, as if I could touch it if I reached out. It was, however, just the accumulated dark energy from the creatures wandering around.

Darkness shrouded the buildings, and dimly lit lamps lined the roads. The streets were surprisingly clean and free of trash. A few vendors were yelling from behind their stalls, selling items regarded as rare or magical. My stomach clenched as we walked by a vendor selling skins from various supernaturals—werewolves included. I exhaled heavily through my mouth and kept walking behind Cyrus as we made our way through the town.

We walked by bars and brothels filled with half-naked women whose calls to the men strolling by echoed in the night like a song. Loud voices from a bar filled with vampires, demons, and even dark elves caught my attention, and a woman's scream pierced the night as a vampire grabbed her and sank his fangs into her throat.

The men and women around the vampire—the other Skins—all laughed as the girl's head lulled to the side, her eyes devoid of life. Two other women walked over and picked up the girl's body, not caring that she'd just been needlessly murdered.

"Keep walking," Cyrus whispered.

What kind of place is this?

I followed Cyrus quietly and did my best not to get distracted by every growl, howl, and scream I heard. I remained close to him and kept my head down, just as he had asked. The stench of death in the air was stifling.

"Help!" A woman's scream met my ears, and as Cyrus turned left to walk down a narrow alleyway, my black eyes fell on a woman being robbed of the items she was selling—a few jeweled necklaces.

"This was where you spent your time learning to control your hunger?"

Cyrus stopped before an iron door before pulling his hood back to reveal his face. "I did. You've only seen the smallest fraction of the market. Specifically, I spent my time in this place." He pointed at the door and then knocked.

A small window of sorts in the center of the door opened and bright green eyes stared out at us. The eyes wandered up and down Cyrus's body before the window slammed shut and the door opened, revealing a seven-foot incubus.

"Welcome back, Cyrus," the incubus said as he stepped aside to let us in. He bowed to Cyrus and my eyes widened a little. I was fully aware that Cyrus was royalty among his kind, but I never really gave it much thought. He was just so normal to Skye and me.

The incubus's eyes scanned me from head to toe, and

somehow, I felt like he was seeing through my cloak to my naked body. "Who's the girl? The boss doesn't like newcomers."

"She's with me," Cyrus answered calmly.

I avoided looking at the incubus. There was just something about his stare that made me feel uneasy. Cyrus said nothing further as he continued walking down a dark corridor, coming to another incubus who stood by a closed door. While the first incubus was massive with a bald head and multiple scars covering his shirtless chest, this one was slender with black hair that was slicked back into a ponytail. He was shirtless like the first one, and he, too, bowed to Cyrus before opening the door and allowing us to enter.

This room was a bar. Candles with blue flames rested on each wooden table and filled the room with an eerie blue light. A woman tended the sizable bar, and dark creatures occupied a few of the tables. At first, it surprised me to see werewolves chatting amongst themselves at one of the tables, but then I realized they must be rogues—werewolves without a pack. I followed Cyrus to the back of the room and took a seat as I observed my surroundings.

I noticed several curious stares as I looked around the bar, but the sight of unusual yellow eyes ogling me was unnerving. The man was sitting alone at the other end of the bar, close to the exit. His hair was as white as snow, much like his skin, and it was so long, it fell over his shoulders. I inhaled the scent drifting from his table and frowned at how sweet it was—like nothing I'd ever smelled before. As the corner of his mouth arched, a chill went down my spine, and I looked away quickly.

"It's best if you don't look at him," Cyrus said in a low

voice as he reclined in his chair. Considering his back was turned to the rest of the bar, I wasn't sure how he knew who I was looking at. "The creatures here aren't friendly."

There were so many beings in this world that I'd never even heard of. Being here with Cyrus now, it suddenly hit me just how dangerous this place was. How dangerous he could be.

"Don't worry. No one here will approach you," he added after a moment. "Not while you're with me."

"They know who you are. Those incubi bowed to you."

He nodded. "They do, although I kept it a secret for a while. But you see how things are around here. Eventually, I had to reveal my wings."

"So, is this like a demon bar or something?"

"Not necessarily. It's a bar that welcomes any being—dark creatures, supernaturals, gods, and demigods. Everyone is welcome here. And many of them come for the special services only the owner can provide."

"What services?" I asked. Suddenly, my attention shifted to the four women who appeared through a door on the left, each carrying a goblet or goblets to a table.

They were all clothed in sheer white dresses, and I realized they were all humans. Gorgeous, identical humans with long brown hair and two-tone eyes—one brown, one blue.

Finally, the woman behind the bar made her way towards our table, her hips swaying seductively and drawing attention with ease. "For a second there, I thought I was seeing things. The great Cyrus has returned to us," the woman said, stopping in front of us. Her blue eyes wandered to me. "I'm Scarlet. And you are?"

"This is Elinor. She's family," Cyrus responded before I

could say anything. Scarlet nodded as she moved a strand of her strawberry-blond hair behind her ear. Scarlet's lips were perfectly plump and naturally red, and she had an adorable sprinkle of freckles across her nose. She was definitely a succubus.

Are all sex demons this good looking?

Her eyes rolled over my face with interest, the same way the incubus had done at the entrance, and for a moment, I felt really uncomfortable. Cyrus and Theanos were the only incubi I'd known, and I'd never met a succubus before. I wasn't sure how to react to the lustful look in her eyes. She chuckled, noticing my discomfort. I glanced at Cyrus, whose face looked as expressionless as it'd been since we arrived.

"So you're Elinor. You're prettier than I imagined." She smiled warmly, and I couldn't help smiling as well. "If you're family to Cyrus, you're family to me."

"Thank you," I told her, and her eyes wandered back to Cyrus.

"Where is Skye? I'm eager to meet the girl that stole your heart." When Cyrus said nothing, she changed the subject. "So, what brings you back to this little piece of hell? I'm guessing you're not here to feed? You don't look pale—that's a good sign."

Cyrus and I shared a look, and he cleared his throat. "No, I'm not here for that. I'm here to see *her*."

Scarlet frowned. "Are you sure you want to do that? You know the price you'll have to pay."

I didn't have a clue what they were talking about, so I remained quiet. No one spoke for a moment as Cyrus and Scarlet studied each other, and I wondered for a moment if they were communicating in some other way. Cyrus nodded after a moment. As two men raised their voices behind her, Scarlet turned away.

One was a rogue werewolf with a large scar along the left side of his long chin. The vampire he was arguing with hissed loudly, and the soft chatter in the bar turned to silence as his pointy claws elongated.

"Give me a minute," Scarlet said as she walked over to both men.

I watched in surprise—and admiration—as she used the side of her hand to hit the vampire behind his neck, knocking him out. As she reached out to grab the vampire before he hit the ground, she punched the werewolf in the face before he even realized it was coming. She knocked him out right away and even managed to catch him by the collar before he could fall.

"Wow," I said under my breath as she dragged both men towards the exit. "She's strong."

"The men by the door aren't the ones who protect this bar —Scarlet is. When I was here, she taught me how to fight," Cyrus said. "She taught me how to control my hunger as well."

"You told her about Skye, huh?" I said with a smirk, and his cheeks immediately turned red. "It's cool. It's nice you told her about me, too, and not just your girlfriend."

"Don't start," Cyrus grumbled. "But yeah, I have her to thank for a lot of what I know."

"So, who is this 'her' you two were just talking about?"

Scarlet suddenly appeared by our table. "Come with me."

We got up and followed her through the door to the left of the bar and entered a dark corridor. With my senses heightened, I had no problem seeing in the dark, and I noted the doors on both sides of the hall as we walked. Unfortunately, I could also hear the sounds coming from behind them.

I tried not to focus on the sexual noises coming from behind those doors. Really, what did I expect? At the Black Souls Market, everything was for sale . . . including sex—consensual or not. It was making me sick.

At the very end of the hall, I saw a staircase, and behind it was a large door with a red doorknob. Scarlet knocked twice and turned to face us, but her eyes were on me. With my cloak pushed over my shoulders and my Guard uniform revealed, she took advantage of the chance to look me up and down.

"Come in," a voice said from behind the door. Scarlet winked at me before she walked away.

Cyrus and I entered a small room. Shelves upon shelves of books lined the walls, and sitting behind a desk by the door was a woman with long white hair and violet eyes. Right away, I knew she was a witch. Her eyes widened with joy when she saw Cyrus.

"Cyrus! My boy!" the old woman yelled as she got up and hurried around the desk to hug him. She was rather short, coming only to Cyrus's chest. "I knew I sensed my favorite little demon." Cyrus hugged her back, but she pulled away quickly and pointed a wrinkled finger at his face. "Two years! You haven't been back in two years. Your rare little visits used to be just barely enough, but then you utterly vanished."

"I'm sorry. I had a lot going on," Cyrus answered. "But I'm here now," he added with a grin, and she rolled her eyes.

"And who might this be?" she asked, turning to me.

"This is Elinor. She's the one I told you about." I looked from the witch to Cyrus. "Elinor, this is Saleem."

I placed my fist over my heart and leaned forward. "It's nice to meet you, Saleem."

"Likewise, firstborn." Her lips curved with a smirk, and for a moment, I was confused about how she knew of me. Of course, Cyrus must have told her. "But Cyrus, your aura . . ." The smile on her lips faltered. "What's wrong?"

Cyrus held out the strand of Skye's hair that he had taken from her hairbrush. "I need you to find someone for me. I'm running out of time."

Saleem's violet eyes examined the strand of hair, and while she didn't actually smile, the joy in her eyes didn't go unnoticed by me. "You know what the price will be, right?"

I glanced at Cyrus quickly to see his jaw tighten. "I know, and I'll pay it."

Alpha Grayson

My fist came down hard on my desk, cracking it and sending all the objects on it flying across the room. Connor was standing quietly by the door as I got up from my chair and stepped over the broken desk to stand by my window. I closed my eyes, inhaling deeply to calm myself.

"Have you told the Luna?" I asked Connor without turning around.

"Not yet," he answered. I opened my eyes to stare at the

stars hanging high above the earth. I could also smell the oncoming rain.

Elinor, why do you never listen to me?

"How long?" I asked as I turned to face him.

"She was spotted leaving with Cyrus over an hour ago. They were heading east."

The office door opened, and Darian walked in. "Alpha, I ordered men to follow them. I figured it would be best to act immediately." Then, through gritted teeth, Darian added, "We should have expected this. She never does as she's told."

Despite Darian and Elinor's constant bickering, I knew he cared for her with the same sisterly love that Connor had for her. Like myself, he'd feared Elinor being accepted in the Werewolf Guard. As a Guard himself, he was fully aware of the things that Elinor had yet to learn, and he worried that she'd unnecessarily put herself in danger. But her eagerness to venture out into the world was apparently stronger than our attempts to protect her. Even with so many people watching over her, she still managed to get into trouble.

First, vampire Bleeders had almost killed her in the woods, and now this.

Her mother is going to kill me when she hears about this.

Running my hands down my face, I groaned. "At this point, I don't know what else to do with Elinor."

My office door flew open, and Clarice—my beautiful Luna—walked in. "Start by sending men after her." I'd been so occupied by my thoughts I hadn't noticed her heartbeat on the other side of the door. "That's all we can do at the moment. Elinor is no longer a child. She's still a little naïve, very stubborn, and still has a lot to learn . . . But she's an adult now. The sooner you accept that, the sooner you'll realize that that's what caused her to go off and do something like this without telling anyone!"

"I knew you'd blame me for this."

Her chest rose and fell as she took a large intake of breath. "I'm not assigning blame to anyone, but you know what I'm saying is true. I've grown tired of this nonsense between you and Elinor! You tricked your only daughter into believing she had a shot at achieving the one dream she's had since she was a child. You arranged for her to fail the Werewolf Guard examination. You had an arranged marriage formed without her knowledge—and mine, too, for that matter." Clarice's eyes changed to black as her face grew red. "You need to stop this, or one day she's going to leave and never come back."

Her eyes grew sad. "You've been pushing her away from both of us. Both of us, Grayson. Of course, she would impulsively go after Skye, even though she's unprepared. But at least she's with Cyrus. He wouldn't let her go with him unless he had a solid course of action or unless he knew something we don't."

I mulled over my Luna's words as I leaned against the wall by the window. Yes, Cyrus had always been the level-headed one in that trio. And yes, they might have learned something that we hadn't yet. Still, I'd surely be having words with Cyrus when they got back.

I nodded to Connor and Darian. They placed their fists over their hearts and bowed to Clarice and then me before leaving.

I crooked a finger at her, and she walked to me slowly. "I'm sorry," I told her as I kissed her forehead. Clarice rarely raised her voice, but whenever she did, it broke my heart. "I'm really sorry."

"I'm not the one who needs to hear that," she mumbled as she rested her head against my chest.

We stood like that in each other's arms for a moment as I pictured my daughter's face. I closed my eyes and said a prayer to the Goddess to protect her, wherever she was, until Darian's men caught up to her.

"The distance between Elinor and me now seems almost too wide to be fixed. I wish I knew when things changed between us. I've been so focused on other things, I just . . . don't know when I lost her."

Clarice wrapped her arm around my waist and placed her chin against my chest, then looked up at me. "It all began when you started trying to control her life." She sighed. "You've never put yourself in her position, have you? Did you ever try to understand the pressure on her shoulders, being the firstborn of an Alpha and a female? She's expected to find her mate, to be a wife, a mother, a Luna. But to do that, she has to suppress her fire as a firstborn. She has to live with the same power that burns in your veins, but because she's a woman, she has to keep that fire tamed. And why? Just to be a Luna? She doesn't want that." She released me and stepped back. "You've been forcing her to find a mate, and now, because she can't, you're forcing her to marry someone who isn't her mate. Are you seeing it now?"

I turned away from her to stare out the window. I knew marrying her off to Elijah would bring about judgment, but I had hoped it wouldn't be as bad as what was being said about her not being able to find a mate. At least she'd marry a highly respected wolf and she'd belong to a powerful pack.

I shook my head. "Everything I've done is to keep her safe. I've only been trying to do what's right for her."

"I haven't forgotten what it felt like to be her age," Clarice said. "I remember decisions being made for me because my parents thought they knew best. Not everything *you* think is right is actually right for her, Grayson." She placed her hand on my shoulder. "We do our best to protect our children, but we can't shield them from everything. You've been doing Elinor more harm than good by trying to protect her."

Thunder rumbled outside, and it started to rain. Clarice wrapped her arms around me from behind, and we stood in silence for a moment as the night sky was lit up by lightning. I, too, remembered being young and wanting things that went against my parents' plans for me. But this was different. Elinor was too reckless. She was going to get herself in trouble, I just knew it.

"I think the final test during the Guard examination really affected Elinor. I-I had no idea anything like that could happen—a girl getting bitten and infected by a vampire? And because Elinor couldn't kill her friend, she failed the test? I wanted her to fail, but I didn't ask for that."

"I know, my Alpha. And deep down, Elinor knows that, too. But a traumatizing event happened to her because of a decision you made." She took a deep breath. "Right now, she's missing, along with Skye and her mother, and we need to focus on that. When Elinor gets back—and she will—you can talk to her about how you want your relationship with her to be."

"If she talks to me," I mumbled. Being an Alpha, I always had to stand firm, not show too much emotion, and remain calm and grounded. But from the moment Elinor was born, she'd always been able to throw me off balance.

Then I smiled, recalling the times when she was a child and would look at me with such love.

"Elinor might be many things, including stubborn—which she got from you, by the way . . ." She tightened her arms around me, and I chuckled. "But she's not a hateful girl. She's angry at you—and not even you can blame her for that—but she doesn't hate you. But . . . do you really think marrying her off to Elijah is a good idea, Grayson?"

"No," I answered softly as I closed the window and turned to face her. "But Elijah is an honorable man, more so than many of the wolves Elinor already met who were only interested in her because she's a firstborn."

"What you are forcing Elijah and Elinor to do is wrong, and you know it. Marrying someone who is not a mate is taboo among our kind for a reason. What will happen if a few years after Elinor and Elijah are married, one of them meets their mate?" She pointed her finger in my face. "What will you do then, hmm?"

I walked around her, my hands behind my back, and stared down at my broken desk. Of course, that thought had crossed my mind. "But I can't have a daughter without a mate, Clarice. She has to have someone around to protect her. Because I won't always be here to do it."

"You're speaking as if you're going to die, Grayson," she said, her voice low with concern.

I shook my head. "I'm just saying I won't be the Alpha forever. Jackson will be the next Alpha, and I want to make sure that whoever Elinor ends up with will take care of her—whether he's her mate or not. Is that so bad? She's a special girl—hell, she's a white wolf—and I know a hard future is waiting for her. I can feel it."

Maybe the conversation I had with Faelen made me more paranoid about Elinor's future than before, but with everything going on, I thought it best to keep that conversation to myself for now. Once Elinor and Skye returned safely, I'd speak to Elinor and have her blood tested for divinity.

Clarice smiled. "Is that why you're so worried about her? Grayson, you still don't give her enough credit, even after seeing how powerful she already is. Elinor doesn't need a mate to protect her. She's strong enough to look after herself." She sighed. "Why don't you tell her what you've just told me? Instead of behaving as if she won't survive without you intervening, just admit that you're a worried father."

She got up on her tiptoes and kissed my cheek. As she pulled away, I picked her up and pressed my lips to hers.

"What would I do without you?" I said, holding her tight.

She smiled at me, but I could see the tears welling in her eyes. *Great.* "I'll get her back," I promised, crushing her to my body again. She rested her head against my chest, her tears soaking my shirt and making my heart ache. "I'll bring our daughter back. But for now, I trust Cyrus to keep her safe."

14

SKYE

There was a bitter taste in my mouth as the darkness in my mind began to fade. Groaning, I slowly raised my hand to press my fingers against my temple. My head was pounding.

A pungent scent burned my nose, and when I opened my eyes, I realized that I hadn't imagined the multiple different heartbeats I'd thought I heard. I sat up slowly and looked at all the humans and supernaturals around me. Men and women, old and young from various species—they were all curled up on the floor or standing in the corners of the dark, dank cell. I closed my eyes for a moment, my head still throbbing, and when I tried to stretch my leg out, I kicked someone in the process.

"Sorry," I mumbled, pulling my leg back up. A torch outside the cell was the only source of light, but I could see well enough, thanks to my werewolf senses. My heart dropped as reality sank in. I hadn't dreamed that attack on Elinor and me—it had all been real. I'd been abducted.

When I saw my mother lying against the wall, I yelled,

"Mother!" Even in the dim cell, I could see well enough to notice a bruise across her cheek. But she was still unconscious.

I crawled over to her and shook her gently. "Mother, wake up."

"She won't wake up," a woman sitting beside my mom's body mumbled. "Not until the magic used to put her to sleep wears off."

"Where are we?" I asked, and the woman's pale blue eyes finally looked my way.

She said nothing, then looked away once more. The smell of death was ripe in the air, mixed with the potent scent of blood and feces. I got up once I felt my strength return to my legs and walked toward the cell's rusted iron bars. I tried to see if there were guards outside the cell, but I saw none. Gripping the iron bars, I inhaled deeply and pulled, then staggered backward in confusion. Even with my enhanced strength, I couldn't break the bars.

I tried repeatedly, but it was as if I was an ant trying to lift a mountain.

"That's no use. Not even a werewolf can break those bars," a man's voice whispered from behind me. I turned around to find the sad gray eyes of a human staring at me. "They've been spelled. They're unbreakable."

He was painfully thin, with sunken eyes and hollow cheeks.

"How long have you been here?" I asked him, and he closed his eyes for a moment.

"I don't remember," he answered.

I glanced at my mother. She was still unconscious, her chest rising and falling slowly.

I need to get us out of here.

"You need to stop moving around so much. You don't want to alert the guards," a woman behind me said in a hoarse voice, but I turned towards the bars, still looking for a way to escape.

My eyes darted around, noting the empty cell just across from ours, and I wondered if there were other cells with people in them. I couldn't hear any more heartbeats other than those belonging to the sixteen or so humans and supernaturals in the cell behind me. I must have been taken by the people Alpha Grayson had told us about.

I glanced over my shoulder, then walked over to my mother and sat beside her. The woman behind me was right. There was no point in drawing unnecessary attention. Eventually, someone would have to appear, and then, if an opening presented itself, I'd act. I wasn't like Elinor—I'd been training to become a pack doctor, not training to fight or protect. But I was still a werewolf.

"What is this place?" I asked the woman sitting beside my mom.

She sighed, her lips dry and cracked in multiple places. "This is where we die," she answered weakly before resting her head back against the wall.

Others inside the cell were crying softly around me, and I bit down on my lip to stop myself from panicking. I closed my eyes, and under my breath, I whispered, "Cyrus and Elinor, please hurry and find us."

Then I remembered that Cyrus had already left. And with that thought, despair set in. If not Cyrus, I knew Elinor and the Alpha would come looking for us. I just hoped they would get here in time.

Elinor

*D*irectly behind Saleem, there was a huge glass shelf filled with jars of various strange things— things like bark, herbs . . . and body parts from a variety of different creatures. Cyrus and I sat in front of her desk as we watched her pick the ingredients for the spell she planned to perform to help us find Skye.

She picked up a jar with what looked like a giant fang in it and placed that on her desk beside the others.

"What's the price?" I whispered to Cyrus as Saleem began removing the ingredients from the jars and placing them in a bowl.

"My blood," Cyrus answered.

I looked at him, confused. I had thought the price would be higher than that, given the way he and Saleem had reacted.

"Just your blood?" I probed, and he nodded.

"Because I'm the Demon King's son, my blood is rare and powerful. In the wrong hands, it could do a lot of harm. But it's the price I have to pay for Saleem's help. A small vial is all I have to give her, but it's powerful enough to both restore her youth and fetch her a good price in the Black Souls Market. Saleem and Scarlet helped me learn to control my power and my cravings. My blood was a small price to pay. I just hate the extraction process."

When he looked at me, he must have noticed my confusion. "I purposefully force my power into my blood. Then it's extracted by an excruciating spell. But my blood becomes even stronger . . . and worth more."

"Oh," I drawled.

"Saleem's trustworthy. The old bat just loves money," Cyrus chuckled, as did Saleem.

"Right you are, my boy. But your blood can triple the strength of any spell." She looked up at us from below her lashes. "That's a good ingredient for a black magic user like myself to have." She removed small red eyes from a jar and dropped them into the cauldron on the desk. Then she held her hand out to Cyrus. "Give me the hair."

Cyrus handed her the strand of Skye's hair. She held it up to her lips, muttered a few words I didn't understand, and then dropped the hair into the cauldron. A blue flame erupted from inside, and she nodded with satisfaction.

"Good." She reached into her bosom and pulled out a thread necklace with a vial attached. "I've been saving this for when you returned."

Cyrus shook his head, seeing the vial of blood around her neck—his blood. "Of course you did."

"So, tell me, what is your relationship to the owner of this hair?" she asked as she emptied the vial into the cauldron. I had to shield my eyes from the brilliant cerulean light that suddenly filled the room.

"It belongs to Skye, our best friend," Cyrus answered. I glanced over at him, noticing his clenched fists. He was barely holding himself together. "Someone took her."

Saleem raised a brow as she considered this information. "Mm, I've heard rumors of supernaturals going missing."

"Do you have any idea who might be behind it?" I asked, but she shook her head.

"No, all I've heard are whispers, and nothing more." Then she motioned us both forward with a finger. "Hold hands. Since she's a friend to you both, the connection will be stronger. One of the humans who worked here vanished a few months ago. Of course, in the Black Souls Market, anything could have happened to her, but Scarlet said all traces of her scent vanished. That has black magic written all over it."

"So witches are responsible for this?" I asked. But Saleem shook her head.

"Not necessarily, darling. Witches aren't the only ones who use black magic. Most people think of witches when they hear about black magic, but demons are the ones that naturally use it. Witches, elves, and many other species can use black magic if they choose to. Even humans can use it. They can either train themselves, sell their souls, or tie themselves to a demon. I trained myself. So, what I'm saying is . . . anyone could be behind these disappearances."

One thing was clear to me—whoever was abducting these people, they had to be powerful to use such strong black magic. I was terrified to discover why they'd need to take so many people. Something was coming, and I had a feeling it was going to be devastating. I just hoped Saleem could locate Skye so we could get her back home before all hell broke loose.

Cyrus held my hand, and I followed his lead, closing my eyes. "Picture Skye in your minds and hold on to that image," Saleem muttered before she began chanting.

Warmth filled the room, and even with my eyes closed, it was as if I could see a flashing light pulsating within the room. I held an image of Skye and me during one of our sleepovers in my mind as Saleem's chant grew louder.

Skye was more than a friend to me—she was my sister. I squeezed Cyrus's hand at the thought that right now she might be in pain, and my wolf stirred within me.

"Breathe," Cyrus said, squeezing my hand. "Focus."

I bit down on my lip, pushing all my negative thoughts away and focusing on memories of us all together. I thought about Skye and Cyrus supporting me during my Werewolf Guard examination and all the times we spent together at our favorite spot in the forest.

I remembered Skye's boy-crazy ways, even though she'd really only had eyes for Cyrus since we were little. I started smiling, thinking about how she always knew when something was wrong with me and wouldn't give up until I told her. Before Cyrus arrived, it had just been her and me, and she'd forever be my sister.

A loud ringing had Cyrus and me covering our ears as we opened our eyes. A blue light emanating from within the cauldron filled the room, and Saleem had stopped chanting. I noticed a crease between her brows, and she seemed to be straining. Then, without warning, the cauldron exploded, throwing Saleem to the side and blowing Cyrus and me back, too.

My back slammed against the door, the sound of the wood breaking echoing in my ear. Cyrus was up in seconds and rushed across the room to help Saleem.

"What was that?" I asked as Cyrus helped her into a chair.

"There is magic, powerful black magic, around your friend." Saleem rubbed a finger against her temple. "I wasn't able to get a location."

Cyrus combed his hair back with frustration. "It's okay. Thank you for trying."

Saleem held her hand up. "There is another way. If another demon would be willing to participate, I might be able to break the spell and find her. The spell's protection faltered for a moment, then pushed back. I'm just not strong enough on my own, and Scarlet won't be strong enough, either."

Cyrus nodded. "Okay, I understand." He turned to me. "Are you okay?"

"I'm fine. Can you think of any other demon we could ask for help?"

He rubbed his knuckles across his cheek thoughtfully for a moment before nodding. "Saleem?" She looked up at him from where she was removing a shard of the cauldron from her wrinkled hand. "Do you have enough strength left to contact someone for me?"

15

ELINOR

I leaned forward, propping myself against the balcony wall as I looked over the Black Souls Market. The cool night air was combing through my hair as I stood on the roof, causing the strands to blow behind me from time to time. I could hear screams off in the distance, but I did my best to ignore them.

Waiting for Theanos to arrive was costing us time, but I knew it couldn't be helped. I'd thought about asking Saleem to contact Will but decided against it when Cyrus suggested his brother. It would be sunrise in a few hours anyway, so Will wouldn't have been able to help. I just felt like the more time that passed, the farther Skye drifted away.

"Hey." Cyrus appeared at my side. "Theanos will be here soon."

I nodded as I kept looking out over the market. "Okay."

"He's never going to let me forget this, but he's the only demon I could ask."

"I just hope we'll be able to find Skye. If not, what other option do we have?"

He shook his head. "There is no other option—at least, not that I can think of right now. This has to work."

"Great," I grumbled. "Then let's keep our fingers crossed." We stood in silence as an enormous creature with wings circled a building top in the distance. "Is that a gargoyle?"

Cyrus leaned forward. "Yes. They're nasty creatures. I fought one once. They have terrible tempers."

Even in the dark, I could make out the creature's curved horns and long arms hanging limply at its side. It grabbed onto the highest point of the building as lightning flashed in the distance.

"Have you given any more thought to what you plan to do about Will?"

"Um," I drawled, caught off guard by that question. "What do you mean?"

"I was thinking about the conversation the three of us had the night Skye was taken. You had decided not to marry Elijah. But what about Will and your father? I know you're going to continue seeing Will, but what will you do if your father finds out? Are you even prepared for what could happen?"

I inhaled deeply and grimaced at the awful scent that drifted up to my nostrils. I turned to the side to lean against the wall.

"I haven't given it much thought, to be honest. I mean, Skye was abducted right after that, and well, we're here. But my guess is that if my father finds out about Will, he'll be really upset and angry with me. He'll tell me I'm making the wrong choice, but he does that all the time anyway.

"But he'll also hunt Will down, potentially starting a war.

And he could even banish you from the pack," Cyrus added. "He won't just get mad."

"I know all of that, Cyrus. Will knows that his kind will be angry if they find out, too. But he made it clear he won't stay away. And I don't want him to."

The massive wings of the gargoyle spread wide before it flew down between the buildings, clearly hunting. Even though we were far away, I still heard a man's cry of agony. I glanced at Cyrus as he looked my way, and I shook my head.

I'm not sure how much more of the market I can take.

"When I found you and Will in the forest and I saw him kiss you without you biting his lips off, I thought I was hallucinating," Cyrus laughed. "I was certain he must have done something to you because no way would the Elinor I knew ever kiss a vampire."

Heat crawled up my cheeks at the memory, and I leaned forward, letting my hair shield my face.

"Oh, hush." I remembered staring at the snowflakes on Will's hair, wondering how a dark creature like him could look so beautiful. "I've been attracted to very few men so far. And while many of them put me to sleep the minute they open their mouth, conversation with Will never gets dull. Not that I'd ever tell him that, the smug bastard. But he is breaking down my defenses." I placed my hand on my chest, patting the flower I'd received in the dragon forest. "We spend so little time together, and after he leaves, I'm never satisfied. He's still such a mystery. I love and hate it."

"Then I think you two need to stop playing around. What's between you has the potential to start a war. Is your friendship worth it? If you're both willing to take such a dangerous risk, admit your feelings to each other and be done with it. Stop drawing this out. He has feelings for you, and you have feelings for him. Admit it. You don't want to be just friends. So you need to decide if being with Will is worth losing your pack . . . or starting a war. Either way, seeing each other in secret will only hurt you both in the end."

I stared at Cyrus for a moment, seeing his eyes darken with anger. "You wish you had told Skye about the way you felt earlier?"

He said nothing, but I knew I was right. Still, I understood what he was saying. I had to decide what I wanted to do, and soon. Above us, the stars looked so close, I was tempted to reach out and see if I could touch one.

"If I married Elijah, I'd be a part of his pack. But if either of us found our true mate, it would cause chaos and pain. I could find myself without a pack if he meets his mate and accepts her, leaving me to go rogue or return to the Blackmoon Pack. And if I met my mate and rejected him in favor of Elijah, I'd risk losing my mind—and maybe my life—just to preserve my marriage. How valuable would I be as a Luna then? I think I'd rather go rogue."

"Are you sure about that?" Cyrus asked.

I nodded. "Not all rogues are plagues on society. Sure, rogue wolves often become thieves or bounty hunters for hire. But even bounty hunters can be helpful for society, depending on the types of jobs they accept. Just because you're a bounty hunter doesn't mean you can't still follow a moral code."

"So you're prepared to become a bounty hunter if you're banished because your father finds out about you and Will?" Cyrus looked utterly surprised.

The thought had briefly crossed my mind before. If my father ever discovered my friendship with Will and I was indeed banished, I wouldn't have a choice in becoming a rogue werewolf. However, at least I would be free to do what I wanted, to be the woman I'd always wanted to be—one who helped others and hunted dark creatures.

"I'd rather be a rogue werewolf than marry Elijah," I said with finality. "If my father wants me gone so badly, then I'll give him that. But it'll have to be on my terms. Then he won't have the right to control who my friends are . . . or who I chose as a partner."

"Hmm," Cyrus said.

I elbowed him. "What? What does that mean?"

"Nothing. As long as you know what you're doing, I'll support you. Now all you have to do is tell Will how you feel and see what he says."

My heart skipped a beat at that. "Can't he just know without me having to say anything? You men need to learn how to read minds."

"I'm afraid we haven't evolved to that level yet."

Cyrus and I laughed for a moment until yet another scream—one that echoed through the night from just below us—snapped us back to reality. I leaned over the balcony, and sure enough, a human woman had her back to the wall as two vampires advanced on her.

My eyes turned black as one of them grabbed her and sank his fangs into her arm. She screamed again, and as she swung her other hand around to hit him, the second vampire grabbed that hand as well.

Within me, my wolf howled with rage. I'd finally had

enough. I couldn't hold back anymore, couldn't stand by and watch as people died all around me.

"Why do these people come here when they know what the Black Souls Market is like?" I growled through clenched teeth.

"Many are born here and have no way of leaving," Cyrus answered, and my resolve to act increased.

I looked at Cyrus, and he sighed and nodded. I grinned as my fangs elongated and the sweet pain of my claws piercing through my fingertips rolled up my arms. I climbed onto the wall, and my howl echoed through the night as I jumped two stories below.

Cyrus

"I'm sorry, brother. But we'll get her back." Theanos pulled me into a hug, and while he'd never hear these words from my lips, I was glad that he came.

"Thanks," I told him as we pulled apart. He hugged Elinor next.

Theanos pulled his long blond hair into a ponytail as he watched Saleem gather the ingredients for the spell. "Let's do this, then. I like Skye, and I'm going to be pissed if she's hurt. But it's weird—I haven't heard anything about supernaturals being taken."

"The supernatural leaders were keeping it a secret for a while. But it's become too much of a problem now to keep silent." I pinched my chin thoughtfully. "I wonder if they took any dragons."

"If a single dragon had gone missing, the Dragon Council would have been notified. But if whoever is responsible for these disappearances manages to take a dragon against their will, well . . ." Theanos inhaled deeply as his lips formed a thin line. "Then there would truly be a reason to panic. First of all, any fight involving dragons would be absolutely chaotic. Secondly, my father isn't known for his good nature. And also, if a dark creature was able to abduct a dragon, even a young one, that creature would have to be incredibly strong to pull it off."

"Let's hope no one tries to take a dragon, then," I said.

Blue light filled the room, and Saleem called Theanos forward. "Theanos, I'm going to need a drop of your blood."

I watched as she pressed a knife against his palm to cut him, only the knife bent. "Oh, ah, sorry," Theanos shook his hand before inhaling deeply and then exhaling. "Try again."

"You're only half dragon, but you inherited their unbreakable skin. Incredible." Saleem's violet eyes were practically glowing with intrigue. "It's fascinating that you can make yourself vulnerable at will."

"Saleem . . ." I drawled, and her grin widened as she moved Theanos's hand so his blood would drip into the cauldron.

"Oh, relax, Cyrus. You'll forever be my favorite incubus."

Blue light erupted from the cauldron, and once my blood and Skye's hair were added to the mix, we were ready to try again.

With Elinor in the middle and Theanos and I standing on

either side of her, we held hands as Saleem began the ritual. After taking a sip of the concoction she had made, Saleem began chanting, and cerulean light filled the room once more. This time, I could feel my energy being pulled towards her, increasing the strength of her spell.

I squeezed Elinor's hand as she moaned in pain. Her energy was probably fading quicker than Theanos's and mine.

"Almost!" Saleem groaned through clenched teeth as a ringing began in the room. "More, boys, I need more! Release Elinor. Do it quickly!"

Theanos and I released Elinor and quickly held hands instead. The moment our hands touched, a burst of power was released. My eyes became red as his blue eyes turned black. Elinor was strong—there was no doubt about that—but this was black magic, something she wasn't used to. With her out of harm's way, we didn't have to hold back. Instead, we combined our energy and then released it.

Saleem's eyes had turned white during our first attempt, but this time, they became black. Only the darkness didn't stop there. It spread from her eyes to her skin. Soon it covered most of her face. A charcoal-colored liquid dripped from her lips, but she continued to chant as she reached up to hold her throat with one hand while the other hovered over her cauldron.

I grew worried about her safety when her skin paled. Theanos and I glanced at each other, about to release each other and end the spell, when Saleem was thrown back against her glass shelf.

"Saleem!"

"I'm fine, Cyrus, I'm fine." The old woman got up quickly,

brushing shards of glass from her shoulder. She wiped away the charcoal-colored substance from her chin before reaching into her mouth and pulling out the strand of Skye's hair that I had given her. Her chest was rising and falling rapidly as her skin returned to its normal color, and she dropped the hair back into the cauldron. "I saw her."

My heart skipped a beat. I stepped forward and placed my hands on her desk. "Where is she?"

"So did I," Theanos added, and Saleem narrowed her eyes at him.

"You piggy-backed on my spell?"

Theanos brushed his hand down the sleeve of his white cotton shirt and grinned at her. I'd forgotten how mischievous he could be. "I wanted to see what you were doing. Besides, this way, I can track Skye myself." He turned to me. "I can find her, Cyrus, but we need to leave now. She was lying in a cell with other supernaturals and humans."

"Thank you, Saleem," Elinor said, stepping forward. "We should get going."

"Wait!" Saleem held her hand up before turning back towards her broken shelf. She looked around for a moment, then picked up a small black bottle. "Here, each of you take a sip. It'll replenish your energy. After all, none of you know what you're about to face."

"Thank you, Saleem." I took a sip of the liquid, relieved that it didn't have a taste. "I'll return with your payment once I've found Skye."

She waved her hand dismissively as Theanos drank next, then Elinor. "Yes, I know you will. I hope you find her and discover who's behind all of this."

After we made our way outside, Theanos removed his

shirt and allowed his wings to emerge from his back. While my wings had red feathers, his were multicolored scales. Being a son of the Dragon King, Theanos's power level nearly rivaled mine.

"Can you tell how far away she is?" Elinor asked him.

"Yes, she's about . . ."

"Wait," I said as a familiar scent drifted to my nose. I turned around to see a cloaked figure at the entrance of the alleyway. It was no doubt a vampire, but its smell wasn't pungent like most others. "How did you find us?"

Elinor's heart rate spiked as she stepped forward, and the shadowy figure moved closer, too.

"I told Elinor I'd find her no matter where she goes," Will answered, removing his hood.

"I knew it," Theanos mumbled beside me, and I turned to him immediately.

"You knew what?"

Theanos waved his hand, his eyes remaining on Elinor and Will as they embraced. "Nothing. I smelled a vampire on her the night of the festival."

And you said nothing to me?

"How did you find me?" Elinor asked Will.

"I have friends everywhere. I heard about what happened to your friend, and I knew you'd do something reckless."

"Life is more fun that way, you know," Elinor replied, and Theanos and I shared a look.

A part of me was still skeptical about Will, but he was looking at Elinor in the same way I looked at Skye—with love. I'd never heard of a vampire capable of feelings such as love—they only felt hunger and lust, as far as I knew. But if

Will had a beating heart, maybe he was the only vampire in existence who had a soul, too.

Vampire or not, I could tell the feelings he had for her were real. I could also understand the strained relationship between them. While I got to spend as much time as I wanted with Skye, Elinor and Will had to settle for brief meetings in the forest.

"Wait, you have blue eyes? That's bizarre. Are you a hybrid or something?" Theanos looked Will up and down, and I closed my eyes at his habit of blurting out the first thing that came to mind. His question was a valid one, though.

"We need to go, Elinor," I added as Theanos's wings flapped loudly beside me.

"Your father has sent Guards after you both." Will reached out and held her hand. "I would come with you if I could. Unfortunately, the sun will soon rise."

"It's okay, we'll be back soon. Um, there are a few things I want to talk to you about," she said.

Will nodded. "Be careful, Little Wolf." Then he pulled his hood over his head as I shifted into my demon form, and Elinor climbed onto my back.

Her heart was hammering away in my ears as her cheeks turned red. "Don't make me come and find you," she said to him.

When he smiled and turned to walk away, I kicked off the ground, my wings propelling me upward. As we flew through the sky to our unknown destination, I readied myself for a fight. No life would be spared when I found whoever had taken my Skye.

"So, your man's a vampire, huh?" Theanos yelled from

ahead of us, and behind me, Elinor's heart began to pound once again.

I smiled at her reaction. Yeah, she was in love. Now I just had to save mine.

Skye, I'm coming.

16

SKYE

My stomach growled loudly as I wrapped my hands around my body. I was so hungry, I felt exhausted and a little dizzy. But I couldn't sleep, not for a second. I needed to stay alert. Four hours ago, a cloaked figure had opened the cell door. The figure dragged out an elf, a human, and a witch and left again.

None of them had returned, and my fear of what might happen here grew.

An hour before that, a human had died. She'd been thin and weak, her body unable to withstand this slow torture any longer. Her body was still in the cell with us. Beside me, my mother looped her hand through mine, her chest rising and falling slowly as she rested her head back against the wall and closed her eyes.

She didn't look scared. In fact, she looked really calm and had appeared that way from the moment she woke up. She hadn't panicked or tried to break the bars as I had. Instead, she just remained seated with her head back against the wall. Her unruffled attitude helped me to calm down . . . until the cloaked figure took those two supernaturals and the human away, that is.

"You don't look afraid, Mother."

"I am, but there is nothing we can do but wait," she mumbled.

"Wait for what?"

"To be rescued . . . or to be the next one taken," she answered. "You do know why they're leaving us in this cell for so long, right?" I shook my head. "To weaken us, of course. That cloaked figure wasn't very big. You could have fought him, although we don't know if he had any special abilities. Even so, abducting so many supernaturals would be troublesome, even with a spelled cage. If everyone here had enough strength and we all worked together, we would've been able to defeat anyone who came into the cell."

Are you searching for me, Cyrus?

I inhaled and leaned back against the wall, sending a prayer to the Goddess to guide Cyrus or Elinor to me. I knew they were searching for me. They had to be.

"It's okay, don't cry," I heard someone whisper, and then sobs met my ears. "You'll be okay," the woman's voice said again. I looked to my right and saw an elf and a child sitting together in the back of the cell.

The little girl's brown hair was matted on one side, and dirt was smeared across her cheek. She looked to be twelve years old, her brown eyes brimming with tears as her bottom lip trembled.

"Don't cry, honey. They might be listening. Don't cry." The elf wiped at the girl's tears and ran a hand down her hair, trying to calm her.

"I want my mother. They took my mother," the human child whimpered.

"Hey kid, stop crying, or they're going to take you next," a werewolf growled, his sunken green eyes turning black with barely-leashed annoyance.

"Leave her alone," I said, and his eyes wandered to me. "She's a child, and she's terrified."

"Do I look like I care? She's making too much noise. We don't want to give our captors any ideas about coming back, because if they do, I doubt they'll be taking just her!" he said.

As I leaned forward, my mother grabbed my arm. Then she shook her head. Fighting amongst ourselves wouldn't solve anything, and we were making more noise than the child. My chest tightened with sadness as the elf pulled the sobbing child in close to her.

"I want to go home. I don't want to die," the girl cried.

I rose to go to her, to offer her comfort, when the sound of a door opening caused me to freeze in my tracks. Heartbeats spiked within the cell as those lying on the ground found the strength to scurry into the corners or to huddle together against the wall. Light streamed into the dark dungeon from the left, and heavy footsteps drew closer. My mother and I huddled together with the rest.

The girl cried louder, her panicked wails echoing around us, and I feared the worst. They would take her.

"Shh, cover her mouth."

The elf covered her mouth quickly as two cloaked figures appeared outside the cell. I swallowed hard, my heart hammering against my chest while my mother clutched my arm. After opening the rusty iron bars, they stepped inside, and everyone turned their heads away. We were like rats cowering in a corner as cats advanced on us. The figures were unmoving, standing just inside the door, when suddenly one disappeared. I blinked rapidly when I saw him reappear further within the cell. Reaching out, he grabbed onto the hair of a human woman. The woman screamed and fought to be released from the gloved hand of her attacker. She shouted, begging for her life and kicking wildly as he dragged her from the cell.

Then the other cloaked figure stepped forward.

Werewolves, humans, and elves moved out of the way, and he came to a stop before the elf with the crying child. He bent down and grabbed the child's arm, and her head fell back as she screamed.

No.

"No, no!" the elf yelled, but the figure just backhanded her across the face.

Her head slammed into the wall and her eyes rolled back as she fell unconscious. I wanted to move, I tried to speak, but I was frozen with fear as the figure held the child up by her throat, her screams turning into gurgling sounds as she choked.

If Elinor had been here, she would have acted. I knew she would have stood up and defended that child, even if the odds were against her.

My eyes filled with tears as the little girl finally stopped clawing at the hand around her throat and her heartbeat slowed down.

I spoke without thinking. "Put her down, you fucking monster!" I rushed forward, my eyes black and my claws brandished with rage.

A chuckle met my ears before the sting of a slap spread across my face, and I fell to the ground.

"Skye!" my mother screamed, but as she rushed towards me, I held my hand up to stop her. I shook my head and tears streamed down her eyes. "Don't do it," she begged me.

"Stay down," the cloaked figure said, and the others within the cell gasped. Had they not heard these monsters speak before?

How could I stand by and watch this happen to a child? My mother and I were the last to arrive here and the only ones with enough strength left to resist. Maybe I was foolish, but if I was going to die here, I wouldn't go down without a fight.

I got to my feet and spat on the ground. Suddenly, the werewolf I had argued with earlier rushed forward, his howl echoing around us. The little girl fell to the ground, but blood splattered across the wall as the figure beheaded the wolf in a flash. Bile rose to my throat.

The world around me grew cold as my mother rushed forward next, her movements almost silent. But she was easily thrown across the room, blood spilling from her mouth as she slammed against the wall hard enough to crack the stone.

Time slowed down as I saw my mother's eyes roll back and she fell to the ground. Fueled by pain and fury, I howled long and hard, trying desperately to listen for her heartbeat.

A gloved hand grabbed the back of my neck from behind. Blinded by panic and rage, I spun around and punched my attacker, then rushed towards my mother, her name a pained cry on my lips. She inhaled deeply as her eyes opened and she regained consciousness.

Before I could get to her, an arm grabbed me around my waist, and another hand covered my mouth as someone dragged me from the cell towards the open door.

"I like this one," the man behind me chuckled when my attempts to bite the hand over my mouth failed.

We stepped through the door, and he threw me onto the ground so hard, the pain of a bone breaking in my arm had me biting down on my lip hard enough to draw blood. The man stepped over me, and I grimaced when my hand slid in a pool of blood as I tried to sit up.

"I want to keep this one," the same voice said as I finally sat up and saw legs dangling in front of me. "She's feisty."

I fell backward, scurrying away the best I could with a broken arm. Scanning the room, I was horrified by the multiple pools of blood on the floor. Goosebumps broke out on my flesh at the sight before me, and my mouth went dry as the man removed his hood.

My empty stomach spasmed as I dry-heaved. I stared at him, unable to look away as I screamed, the sound ripped from my mouth in terror as the man—no, the creature—stepped towards me.

"Now," the man drawled, "Let's do something about that attitude of yours."

Elinor

We flew for three hours straight before Theanos finally descended. We landed on the outskirts of an abandoned town, and I watched as Theanos bent down and dug his hand into the soil.

"I'm not picking up any life here." He stood up and brushed the dirt off his hand. "There's no aura or heartbeat, but I can feel Skye here."

"Let's go, then." Cyrus walked away, his wings vanishing, and I followed close behind him.

As the early morning sun beamed down on us, the abandoned town appeared to be in worse shape than it had seemed from above. Some buildings had crumbled walls, some had missing doors and windows, and others were just walls where a house had once stood. Trees grew haphazardly throughout the town, proof that the forest was slowly reclaiming the land.

"This town is the perfect location to keep a group of hostages because it's in the middle of nowhere. But I don't get where she and the others could be because there's also nowhere to hide here. All the buildings are ruined," I said as I stepped over a child's broken doll.

"Do you still feel her?" Cyrus asked Theanos when we stopped walking. Theanos nodded and took the lead.

"Yeah, she's up ahead." He pointed to a house with broken windows. "In there."

My eyes changed to black, and Cyrus's changed to red. Our steps were silent as we approached the house. We all knew that just because Theanos hadn't detected anyone, it didn't mean there was no one there. After all, we knew nothing about whoever had taken Skye, so we couldn't let our guard down for a minute.

Cyrus waved his hand to Theanos and me, signaling for us to wait as his wings appeared and he flew above the house.

He dived downward, breaking through the roof, and I growled as I ran forward. We were doing this together for a reason. No matter how strong he might be, rushing in like that was a horrible idea.

"Right now, Cyrus isn't thinking about his safety." Theanos shook his head as we waited for a signal for Cyrus.

"He won't do Skye much good if he gets hurt trying to save her," I pointed out. Moments later, the door to the house opened and Cyrus called us forward. "What the hell was that?" I asked.

Ignoring me, he turned and walked back into the house. "Do you feel her?" he asked Theanos. "Are you sure you feel her here?"

"Yes. When Saleem added her hair to the spell, it created a link of sorts. I know she's here."

"Unfortunately, there is nothing here," I said, bending down and picking up the broken leg of a chair. "No one has been here in a very long time."

Broken furniture was scattered on the ground, along with vines that had snuck in through the cracked windows and were now running across the floors and up the walls. Theanos held his hand out as he turned in a circle. I stood up, spotting a door just across the room, but as I stepped forward, a loud creak came from under my foot.

All three of us froze, and I took my foot off the old rug I had stepped on. Theanos walked forward, his hand still outstretched. His lips pulled up into a smile as he bent down and pulled the rug away, revealing a hidden door.

"There it is." He held onto a piece of rope attached to the door and pulled it up while Cyrus waited, his hands out in case of an attack, fire dancing on his fingertips.

But nothing jumped out at us, except for a horrible smell that had me stepping away fast. "Goddess, what's that smell?"

"Death," Theanos replied as he jumped into the hole in the ground. Balls of fire appeared in both of Cyrus's hands, and he went in after Theanos.

We landed in a room that was dark and damp. "It's a dungeon," I whispered as we looked around at the burnt-out torches lining the walls. "Theanos?"

"Follow me, come on." His wings lit up, providing additional light as we turned left and then right. We came to a point with two entrances and then turned right again.

The tunnels we were walking through were dark and cramped, forcing us to walk in single file. The torches on the rocky walls were out, but judging from the smoke I could see rising from one of them, they'd been blown out recently. I clenched my fists, hoping we weren't too late.

The more we walked, the stronger the smell of blood became—and the more I worried. Maybe they had realized we'd used a spell to locate Skye and had quickly changed locations.

"Damn it," I growled under my breath as we found a corridor with cells on both sides. I wiggled my nose as I walked forward and looked into the cell Cyrus and Theanos were staring into.

My hand flew to my mouth at what I saw before me. I turned away, my jaw tightening, but the horror I'd seen had already imprinted itself in my brain. Mangled bodies were scattered on the floor of the cell. It looked as if a wild animal had gotten loose and ripped everyone to shreds.

I looked in another cell and found that, while there were no bodies, the floor was stained with blood.

"What the hell happened here?"

"I feel her behind there," Theanos said, pointing to a door at the end of the dungeon.

Cyrus wasted no time moving toward the door, his hands clenched at his sides. No doubt he had been looking through the bodies on the ground, searching for Skye or Ms. Clementine, but I couldn't handle seeing the gruesome state of the bodies.

If I'd made it into the Werewolf Guard, I would've had to face things like this, and if I became a bounty hunter someday, I probably would then, too. But my mind just hadn't hardened itself against such sights yet. The Guard examination had been brutal and gory, but nothing like this.

Cyrus's body turned to smoke as he neared the door, and I watched as he passed right through it. Theanos and I stood still, ready to act at any moment. I strained my ears to listen for any sound coming from behind the door, but there was nothing. The more seconds that ticked by, the more anxious I grew.

Was Skye here? Deep down, I knew the answer. This place was abandoned. But had they taken her with them . . . or were she and Ms. Clementine dead? I swallowed hard.

"Come on, Cyrus," I growled under my breath.

I walked along with Theanos. We pushed forward then black smoke seeped through the door and Cyrus materialized before us once more. My tense shoulders relaxed, but I was suddenly overcome with a sadness so strong, it felt like my chest was caving in and squeezing my heart. Cyrus's eyes were red—not from his demon, but from tears he was desperately trying to hold back.

He held his hand up, and I looked away, my eyes squeezing shut. "No, no! She can't be!"

Cyrus's heartbeat sounded like horses galloping in my ears. He stepped back, falling against the door hard. He looked the way I felt—terrified and lost. Because hanging from his clenched fist were Skye's black curls, attached to a chunk of her flesh.

"Where is she?" I cried. "That's just—that's just her fle— Where is the rest of her? And where is Ms. Clementine?"

Cyrus shook his head, his body visibly shaking. "Their bodies aren't here."

But Will and I *can't stay away* from each other.

How could I have fallen for a man I'll **never** get to be with?

To make matters worse, supernaturals and humans are vanishing…

And the number of disappearances are growing.

How did I get dragged into that you might be wondering?

My best friend was taken and even her **SCENT** vanished from the world.

The only question now is,

…will I find her

…before she turns up dead?

https://ssbks.com/BW3

As the son of our village's shaman, I'm expected to marry a virgin bride. But I only have eyes for pregnant widow Ava, who is off-limits for me.

And because life isn't twisted enough, I get another curveball thrown at me...

Plagued by a dark vision, my father binds my soul to my body in an attempt to save me from the worst of what might await. But I'm not relying on a ritual to save myself--I'm going to find out what he saw... and stop it.

Soon I come to realize there's no way I'll get out of this mess alive.

When vampires attack our village, the vampire Queen offers me a terrible choice--one with implications for more than just the survival of Ava and the rest of my clan.

If I give into the Queen's demands, I'll spend an eternity of darkness at her side as the very thing I despise most. With everything and everyone I love at stake, I'd gladly give my life to save my village.

But can I condemn the rest of the world to the monster I'll become?

This is the prequel to the Bloodmoon Wars series.

Are you wondering how Will became a vampire? Click

below to get your FREE copy of the <u>The Dark Ages</u> (Bloodmoon Wars Prequel)

https://ssbks.com/BWPrequel

ALSO BY SARA SNOW

THE LUNA RISING UNIVERSE

THE BLOODMOON WARS (A PARANORMAL SHIFTER SERIES PREQUEL TO LUNA RISING)

The Dark Ages (FREE Prequel)

https://ssbsks.com/BWPrequel

The Awakening (Book 1)

https://ssbks.com/BW1

The Enlightenment (Book 2)

https://ssbks.com/BW2

The Revolution (Book 3)

https://ssbks.com/BW3

The Renaissance (Book 4)

https://ssbks.com/BW4

The New Age (Book 5)

https://ssbks.com/BW5

LUNA RISING SERIES (A PARANORMAL SHIFTER SERIES)

Luna Rising Prequel (Free Download)

https://ssbks.com/LunaPrequel

Luna Rising (Book 1)

https://ssbks.com/LR1

Luna Captured (Book 2)

https://ssbks.com/LR2

Luna Conflicted (Book 3)

https://ssbks.com/LR3

Luna Darkness (Book 4)

https://ssbks.com/LR4

Luna Chosen (Book 5)

https://ssbks.com/LR5

WOLF REBORN SERIES (A PARANORMAL SHIFTER SERIES) - NATALIE'S SERIES

Enchanted Reborn (Free Prequel)

https://ssbks.com/WRPrequel

Wolf Reborn (Book 1)

https://ssbks.com/WR1

Wolf Burdened (Book 2)

https://ssbks.com/WR2

Wolf Scorned (Book 3)

https://ssbks.com/WR3

Wolf Fallen (Book 4)

https://ssbks.com/WR4

Wolf Embraced (Book 5)

https://ssbks.com/WR5

THE VENANDI UNIVERSE

THE VENANDI CHRONICLES

Demon Marked (Book 1)

https://ssbks.com/VC1

Demon Kiss (Book 2)

https://ssbks.com/VC2

Demon Huntress (Book 3)

https://ssbks.com/VC3

Demon Desire (Book 4)

https://ssbks.com/VC4

Demon Eternal (Book 5)

https://ssbks.com/VC5

THE DESTINE UNIVERSE

DESTINE ACADEMY SERIES (A MAGICAL
ACADEMY SERIES)

Destine Academy Books 1-10 Boxed Set

https://ssbks.com/DA1-10

ENJOY THIS BOOK? I WOULD LOVE TO HEAR FROM YOU...

Thank you very much for downloading my eBook. I hope you enjoyed reading it as much as I did writing it!

Reviews of my books are an incredibly valuable tool in my arsenal for getting attention. Unfortunately, as an independent author, I do not have the deep pockets of the Big City publishing firms. This means you will not see my book cover on the subway or in TV ads.

(Maybe one day!)

But I do have something much more powerful and effective than that, and it's something those publishers would kill to get their hands on:

A <u>WONDERFUL</u> bunch of readers who are committed and loyal!

Honest reviews of my books help get the attention of other readers like yourselves.

If you enjoyed this book, could you help me write even better books in the future? I will be eternally grateful if you could spend just two minutes leaving a review (it can be as short as you like):

Please use the link below to leave a quick review:
https://ssbks.com/BW2

I LOVE to hear from my fans, so *THANK YOU* for sharing your feedback with me!

Much Love,

~Sara

ABOUT THE AUTHOR

Sara Snow was born and raised in Texas, then transplanted to Washington, D.C. after high school. She was inspired to write a paranormal shifter series when she got her new puppy, a fierce yet lovable Yorkshire Terrier named Loki. When not eagerly working on her next book, Sara loves to geek out at Marvel movies, play games with her family and friends, and travel around the world. No matter where she is or what she is doing, she can rarely be found without a book in her hand.

Or Facebook:
    Click Here
    https://ssbks.com/fb
    Join Sara Snow's Werewolf Council:
    https://ssbks.com/fbgroup